The Unraveling of Dan Carr

From the Quietus Files

Neal R. Minor

M. LiClar Publishing Co., LLC
Monroe City, MO

ISBN-13: 979-8-9902673-2-9

Disclaimer

This book is a work of fiction. Names, characters, places and incidents are a product of the author's imagination or are used fictitiously. Any resemblance to actual events or locales or persons, living or dead, is entirely coincidental.

ACKNOWLEDGMENTS

Thank you to everyone who read, critiqued and most importantly, bought my first book. Writing and publishing books has been quite a learning experience. I've become addicted to writing and I 'need' to get words, thoughts and ideas out of my head and down on paper. I look forward to hearing your thoughts on my latest creation. Positive and negative feedback is always welcome. All of it helps me grow as a writer.

I

"Mr. Carr."

"Mr. Carr."

"Mr. Carr, can you hear me? If you can hear me, squeeze my hand."

Dan Carr tried to open his eyes, but his eyelids were too heavy. He didn't have the strength to open them. He tried to squeeze the hand, but again, he couldn't muster the strength. He had no idea who was talking to him. All he knew was that he was supposed to be dead. He wasn't sure if he was in heaven or hell, but this wasn't what he imagined either place would be like. He knew he was lying on his back. He knew there was a bright light directly above his head. He knew that the voice had a foreign accent that he was unfamiliar with. He was conscious of the fact that he didn't know where he was but was unable to comprehend exactly what that meant. The smell of antiseptic was thick in the air; it was nauseating.

Without really being awake he knew he wanted to go back to sleep. Was that possible? Could he sleep in heaven? Could he sleep in hell? Maybe a short nap was all he needed and when he woke, he would have a better grasp on the situation.

"Day two post-op. Mr. Carr is still unresponsive and continues to be in a vegetative state. Need follow up with social services to see if contact with a family member has been made." Dr. Khanzada clicked off his recorder and exited the room.

II

"Mr. Carr."

"Mr. Carr, if you can hear me, please squeeze my hand."

Dan Carr was enjoying a wonderful dream when he was startled semi-awake once again by the foreign accent asking him to squeeze his hand.

"I've had about enough of this shit." He thought to himself.

"Either give me my wings or stoke the fires because I can't imagine that anything is worse than this purgatory I'm in now. Every time I get into a wonderful dream about being back on the beach, swimming in the South China Sea, sipping Mai Tais, surrounded by gorgeous Filipino women, some asshole wakes me up and asks me to squeeze his hand

"I wish I could squeeze it so hard that I could break it. Then maybe he'll leave me alone."

Dan strained his eyes to open. The light above his head was blinding. It penetrated his closed eyelids and disrupted what little sleep he got. Trying to open his eyes allowed the blinding light to seep deep within his skull and trigger a flurry of activity. It was too much. The pain felt like a horrible hangover, and he gritted his teeth and clenched his fists.

"Day three post-op, patient's eyelids fluttered, and slight movement was felt in his hand. No update from social services," Dr. Khanzada said into his recorder.

III

"Mr. Carr."

"Mr. Carr, if you can hear me, please squeeze my hand."

"No! No! No, I'm not going to let this prick ruin it. I'm going back to where I was. The first time I met her. She was stunning and I was immediately in love. I don't care if it was just a dream. It was real to me, and I want to go back. Just the thought of the first time I met her had emotions and feelings coursing through this old body that I haven't felt in nearly five decades. Please, just let me enjoy the moment."

Dan struggled to open his eyes. The light pierced all the way to the center of his brain and ignited the pain once again. But he had to confront his tormentor. He had to have closure, one way or the other. How long could purgatory last?

He saw the outline of a dark figure; a shadow of a man hovered over him. The man with the foreign accent? God? Satan? It was impossible to tell, but most likely the voice belonged to the shadow and the hand in his was certainly attached. He squeezed as hard as he could and felt a squeeze back.

"That's good Mr. Carr. I think you are making progress. If you understand what I'm saying, blink your eyes."

"Blink my eyes! What the hell are you talking about? I don't even know if my eyes are open. I don't know if I'm awake or asleep.

I can't discern dreams from reality. All I know is that I want this to end. I want to rest. I need closure."

"Day four post-op. Patient is continuing to show progress. Has opened eyes and looked toward me and squeezed hand. Is trying to form words. A potential family member has been located," Dr. Khanzada said into his recorder as he exited the room.

IV

"Mr. Carr."

"Mr. Carr, it's good to see your eyes. How are you feeling today?"

"How am I feeling? Where do I start trying to answer that question? This morning, I realized that I'm not dead. I'm in a goddamn hospital. I survived. How in the hell did I survive a 9mm in my mouth?

"The sensation of pain that can only be felt by the living has returned. It envelops my head and is relentless. The rest of my body feels fine; except for what I can only imagine is a catheter, which burns like I imagined the furnaces of Hades might feel. Other than that, shadow-voice, I feel great. How are you?"

"Please don't try to speak Mr. Carr. You have a tube in your throat that has been breathing for you and keeping you alive. I think we're going to remove the tube later today. I'm not exactly sure what our next steps will be, but I want your input on our course of treatment.

"I also want to let you know that your son has been contacted. The social worker will be by later to discuss that with you."

"My son? Which son? How in the hell did you contact one of my sons? I have no family. I have no child who cares that I'm here."

V

"Good morning Mr. Carr. I understand that you don't care for the food that the speech therapist has been trying to feed you. You have to understand that if you don't eat, we can't take the feeding tube out of your stomach."

"I don't know who the hell you are, but I have one question for you.

"Are you the reason that I'm alive?"

"Mr. Carr, your throat is going to take a few days to heal. In the meantime, it's going to be very difficult to speak. I know you are trying to talk to me but give it a few days and then I will be able to understand you.

"Dr. Ishtar sent your charts over. Why did you stop treatment? You were making progress. Social services have been by to see you, yes? They have informed you of the situation with your son?"

"Listen here asshole! I have no son, or daughter for that matter, who gives a shit that I'm here. Yes, social-fucking-services told me that they spoke with someone who confirmed that they carried my DNA, but that they weren't authorized to direct my medical care.

"That's right asshole! No one is going to show up to sympathize with you. I HAVE NO ONE! It's just me. You have to deal with me. And just wait until my throat heals. If you think that poor little

speech therapist had a hard time trying to feed an invalid mute, just wait until I can talk, asshole.

"By the way, where in the hell did you get your medical degree and what third world country am I in? Last time I checked guys with an accent like you were the enemy and my country did everything we could to keep your brown ass out."

"Okay Mr. Carr. You will try to eat, and you will try to rest? You are making good progress. Dr. Ishtar may come by to see you to discuss resuming treatment."

VI

"Good morning Mr. Carr. I'm glad to hear that you are trying to eat a little. I know it doesn't have much taste, but it's very important to your recovery that you are able to eat on your own."

"Doc." Mr. Carr garbled.

"Yes, Mr. Carr. It's good to hear your voice."

"Where am I?"

"Yes, Mr. Carr. You are at the University of Virginia Hospital in Charlottesville, Virginia Mr. Carr. Do you know why you are here?"

"I'm guessing that I'm here because I failed to kill myself and you're the asshole that saved me."

"No, Mr. Carr. I didn't save your life. The ER physician and the neurosurgeon saved your life; I'm just trying to help you recover."

"Well, it's a waste of time and resources. As soon as I'm able; I'll do it again and the next time I won't fail."

"Mr. Carr, I don't understand. Dr. Ishtar's chemotherapy was working. The cancer treatment was going well. Why would you want to kill yourself?"

"Dr. Whateverthehellyournameis, with all due respect, I'm

not going to discuss this with you. I have no idea who you are or why you're wasting your time trying to help me recover. I've already told you that as soon as I'm able, I'm going to finish the job that I started. I don't want to see Dr. Ishtar and I'm not going to resume his chemotherapy.

"I have rights, don't I? Can't I refuse any further treatment? You've already kept me alive against my wishes. Why should it be so goddamned hard for someone to die?"

"Mr. Carr, my name is Dr. Khanzada. The only thing we are currently doing to keep you alive is feeding you through a tube in your stomach. You have a right to have it removed, but starvation is a very slow and agonizing death. Perhaps a visit with the Social Services to discuss…"

"No! I don't want to visit with the fucking Social Services! I don't want you to discuss my desire to die. I want this goddamn tube out of my stomach, and I want to be released from this fucking hospital so I can go home and kill myself!"

"Mr. Carr, there's no need for profanity. You do have rights, and this hospital will adhere to those rights, but we also have policy that we have to follow."

"Listen asshole, I don't know who you are or what third world county you're from, but if you're not willing to remove this tube from my gut and release me, then I don't have a need to ever see you in this fucking room again."

"Mr. Carr, my name is Dr. Khanzada. I was born in Pakistan and attended medical school at the University of Virginia. The feeding tube can be scheduled to be removed when the Speech Therapist begins making progress with you. You have to be able to eat on your own or you won't be able to consume enough calories…"

"I don't think you understand what I'm saying Dr. Pakistan. Either you remove the feeding tube and release me from the hospital, or I'm going to rip it out and walk out the door."

"Mr. Carr, you are in no shape to be walking. Physical Therapy hasn't even been able to evaluate you to..."

"Doctor, I'm prepared to die. I don't give a shit about Physical Therapy, and I don't think your primitive, third-world brain can comprehend what I'm saying, so get the hell out of my room. I either talk to an American doctor who has some common sense and understands English, or I'm walking out the door by the end of the day."

Dr. Khanzada turned and walked out of the room. Dan Carr had a smug look on his face that he hadn't had in quite some time. He had the upper hand in the situation, and he knew it. Maybe it would be fun to play this game for a day or two before he continued getting on with ending his life.

VII

Dr. Khanzada went to the nurse's station and called down to the chaplain's office. Fr. Viloria answered the phone.

"Chaplain's office, this is Fr. Viloria. Can I help you?"

"Fr. Viloria, this is Dr. Khanzada, I have a patient that needs some counseling. Not meaning to disrespect you, but is there a Caucasian chaplain on duty today?"

"No Dr. Khanzada, I am the chaplain on duty until tomorrow morning. Is it something that should wait? Does the patient request a particular denomination? Rev. Wheat is on back-up call."

"I don't know that it can wait until tomorrow, Father. I have a patient who is very adamant that he wants to die. He was very hostile toward me and part of the reason is because we are keeping him alive, but he also doesn't want to speak with a foreigner. I would hate to send you into that situation."

"Dr. Khanzada, I understand the situation. I will be happy to call Rev. Wheat but there is no guarantee that he will be available to come in tonight.

"Dr. Khanzada, given the grave nature of the situation and the fact that it's time sensitive, would you allow me an opportunity to visit with the patient? If he does decide to follow through with his wishes, I would prefer that he is as prepared as possible to continue on his journey."

"Fr. Viloria, as a foreign-born individual, I honestly think that you would be walking into a bad situation, but if you really think that you're up to it and you can help, then please go see Mr. Carr in room 514."

VIII

"Good evening Mr. Carr. I'm Fr. Viloria. I understand that you are prepared to have all life-saving measures halted?"

"Are there any goddamn white people working in this hospital? I was in Virginia when I tried to kill myself and I woke up in friggin' Timbuktu."

"Mr. Carr, you are still in Virginia. Dr. Khanzada thought that since you have refused further treatment and your death is imminent, you may wish to speak with a hospital chaplain while there is still time."

"That's what Dr. Pakistan thinks huh?

"And what part of Asia are you from Padre? I used to get paid by the U.S. government to kill you bastards you know."

"Mr. Carr, I don't think the United States has been at war with the Philippines during our lifetime. I grew up there but have lived in the States for over 30 years."

"Philippines huh? I spent a little time there during the Vietnam War. Does your family still sell monkey kabobs on the street corner Padre?"

"Well, my father was an engineer, and my mother was a grade school teacher Mr. Carr, but I'm almost positive that I've eaten my share of monkey in my lifetime. By the way, what did you think of the monkey kabobs?"

"In all honesty, they were a hell of a lot better than the crap my own government served me most of the time. Where in the Philippines are you from?"

"I was born on Mactan Island, and my parents moved our family to Manila when I was very young. I entered the seminary right out of high school and came to the U.S. when I was 20 years old. I've been here ever since."

"Oh, I guess the Philippines is a pretty big place with a lot of people. I met a girl there when I was in the Navy. Haven't seen her in over 50 years. I thought maybe you might know her."

"Well Mr. Carr, the Philippines has nearly 100,000,000 people, so it's highly unlikely I would know her. But, do you remember her name?"

"Of course, I remember her name. Malaya is the mother of my first-born child."

"And where are Malaya and your child today?"

"I said, I haven't seen Malaya in over 50 years. She's dead as far as I know.

"I never met the kid. I only know that it existed and would be about 50 years old, if he or she is still alive."

"Do you have other children Mr. Carr?"

"There's kids running around that have my DNA. I guess you'd call them my children, but I've never had much to do with raising them."

"How many children do you have?"

"Seven that I'm aware of; including the Filipino kid. Could be a few more that I never knew of."

"Are you close with your children?"

"Listen here Padre. I just said that I never had much to do with raising my kids. I was married to a few of their mothers for a few years at a time, but never long enough to get to know my kids…and they don't know me. So, tell those Social Services twats to quit trying to contact people. No one's going to come intervene on my behalf. That's not the way me and my kids operate."

"Well, how exactly do you operate with your children Mr. Carr? Help me understand how you have no one."

"Well, Padre, this is how we operate. I provide a little DNA and when the relationship with their mother breaks down, I hit the road. Except for Malaya, I would have stayed with her forever."

"What happened with Malaya? Why haven't you seen her in over 50 years?"

"That's enough questions for today, Padre. Get this tube out of my gut and I'll talk to you more tomorrow."

"Mr. Carr, I can't make the decision to remove your feeding tube."

"Well, you tell Dr. Pakistan that if he doesn't remove it then I'm going to rip it out. I should be dead by now, but some asshole got involved who should have been minding his own business. So, now they send you in here to try to talk me out of dying by bringing up shit that happened a lifetime ago, but it doesn't matter, I'm here to die; one way or the other."

"Mr. Carr, don't pull the tube out before tomorrow. I'll talk to Dr. Khanzada. And I'm not here to talk you out of dying. I'm just here to help you prepare for death."

IX

"Mr. Carr. I understand from Fr. Viloria that you wish to end all life saving measures."

"Yes, Dr. Pakistan, I told you that yesterday. The Padre seems to be the only one around this joint that understands that I'm serious. He asked me not to yank the tube out last night. That's why it's still in, but I promise you; today, either you remove it, or I will."

"Mr. Carr, I have consulted with Dr. Ishtar. He feels that your chemotherapy was going very well and that it can be continued soon with a full recovery possible."

"Doctor, are you fucking stupid or just plain ignorant? Do you understand that I put a 9mm in my mouth and pulled the trigger? Does that sound like a son-of-a-bitch who wants to continue chemotherapy'?"

"I guess I don't understand Mr. Carr. If chemotherapy was working, why would you quit the treatment and try to kill yourself?"

"Because I'm tired of living and I'm ready to die!

"Why is that so fucking hard to understand Doc?"

"It just doesn't seem like the decision that a rational person would make Mr. Carr."

"Oh, I'm rational Doc. I'm the most rational person you've ever met. I know without a doubt that I'm ready to die. Now, get this fucking tube out of my stomach so I can get on with the process."

"You're positive?"

"Abso-fuckin-lutely!"

"Is there any chance that you would like to speak with a psychiatrist prior to having the tube removed?"

"I'm an equal opportunity asshole. If you want me to throw some insults at a shrink, I'd be happy to do it, but it's not going to change my mind."

"It will be removed later today."

X

"Mr. Carr, I understand that the procedure is complete, and you are only here for comfort measures?"

"Yep, Padre. Seems kind of stupid considering I have no intention of ever paying the bill for this joint and even if I did want to pay it, I don't have the money."

"At the end of the day Mr. Carr, this facility isn't about payment, it's about saving lives."

"You're pretty damn funny Padre. Do you honestly believe that crap?"

"Yes, Mr. Carr, I do. I've seen it during my service here. Money doesn't matter, only healing."

"Well, then this is a one-of-a-kind joint. There's not a non-profit hospital that I know of that doesn't care about the bottom line. Maybe my last kid should have been born here instead of in South Carolina. The hospital over there is still trying to collect $6,000 from me and the kid is probably in his 20s by now."

"What do you mean probably in his 20s, Mr. Carr?"

"I mean, I never met the bastard. I just heard he was mine and I owed the hospital some money. Never had any blood work or anything. Just hooked up with this chick and next thing I know I'm getting hospital bills for a birth that I had nothing to do with."

“Mr. Carr, tell me about your children.”

“What is there to tell? Supposedly I have six or seven little brats running around carrying on my DNA, who don’t know me and don’t want to know me. I’m sure each of them would prefer that I never existed.”

“But if you never existed then they would never exist. Do you know for a fact that’s how they feel about you?”

“Why would they feel any different? I was a druggie coming home after the war. Then the government made it too hard to get drugs, so I switched to alcohol, with the occasional joint when I could score one. I worked just enough to pay the rent and stay drunk. Every time I walked in a bar I could walk out with a chick if I wanted to. That’s the kind of women that birthed my kids…except for Malaya, of course.

“Padre, I’m getting ready to die. What do I have, three, maybe four days, tops? Why are you sitting in here talking to me?”

“Mr. Carr, you have chosen to die by starvation. Despite the very treatable cancer that you have, and the bullet that you shot through your head, you are a mostly healthy man. Starvation can take weeks, possibly a month for a man in your condition. Your cancer certainly won’t take you before starvation and your self-inflicted wounds haven’t caused any permanent, life-altering conditions.”

“Well Padre, it sucks that I missed with that shot. I qualified as an expert marksman in Navy basic training. As my strength comes back, I can promise you that I’ll come up with a quicker solution than starvation. Weeks and months aren’t on my agenda.”

XI

"Good morning Mr. Carr. How are you feeling today?"

"Honestly Padre, I'm a little hungry. Do you think you could fetch me some biscuits and gravy?"

"Mr. Carr, if you would like to eat, I will get you whatever you want."

"I'm bullshitting you. I'm not hungry and even if I was, I wouldn't eat. I'm here for one thing, and that's to die."

"You know, Mr. Carr. As the days go by without any nourishment in your body, you will become weaker and weaker. Your plan to find a way to kill yourself before you starve is going to become more and more difficult the longer you go without food."

"You're a smart one Padre. You catch on quick. I don't even have the strength in my legs to get out of bed or move much of anything. Otherwise, I would have already sealed the deal.

"Don't worry, I'll get it figured out."

"Mr. Carr, you've mentioned Malaya and your child with her several times. Can you tell me more about that?"

"Well, what do you want to know? My time with Malaya was the last time that I was ever happy, if that tells you anything."

"How did you meet her?"

"Well, I was a young man in the Navy. I had run away from a bad situation at home and after spending a few years bumming around and nearly starving to death, I forged a few documents and joined the military at age 16 and was sent to Vietnam. I was a pretty crappy student when I was in school and didn't really have any skills to speak of, so I figured I'd let Uncle Sam give me three hots and a cot for a few years. I was a pretty dumb kid, but I knew enough to know that with the path I was on, it was either going to be the military or jail."

"So, you ran away from home? Tell me about that."

"I thought you wanted to know about how I met Malaya. Make up your mind Padre."

"Mr. Carr, I don't see that you have anything better to do for the next few weeks than tell me stories, so why don't you begin at the beginning."

"The beginning of what?"

"How about the beginning of your life?"

XII

"I was born in the late spring or early summer of 1946 on a small farm in Central Iowa. I don't remember the exact date, but I remember that mama always made me a little cupcake sometime after school was out for the year. When I joined the military, I decided that I liked May 31st, so that's been my birthday ever since. I was born at home in a two-room shack that my daddy had built himself. My daddy was quite a bit of an alcoholic and drinking was really the only thing he was ever very good at. He sure wasn't very good at building houses.

"We share cropped about 50 acres, including five acres of timber that daddy called the draw. The draw separated the two tillable fields and was my escape from daddy's belt. From the time I could reach the latch on the front door, I spent as much time as possible in the draw.

"When I was six my twin brothers were born, but daddy took mama to the hospital in Ames to have them. That was the first time I remember mama leaving the farm for any reason.

"Daddy left me at home because we had a ewe that was lambing. I was only six, but I'd helped pull lambs plenty of times and I knew that daddy expected healthy lambs when they got back.

"That was also the first time in my life that I ever remember being scared. We didn't own a vehicle yet, so daddy hitched up the horses and put mama in the wagon and he looked me in the eye and said, *"Boy, I'm expecting you to take care of the place while we're gone. We may be a day or two. Take care of the sheep and take care of the house."*

"That's quite a bit of responsibility to put on a six-year-old Mr. Carr."

"Things were different then Padre. We grew up a hell of a lot faster. I wasn't scared to take care of the sheep and the house. Hell, I think I probably could've taken care of the whole farm better than my drunk daddy. I remember standing in the front yard and watching the wagon roll away and my mama looked back over her shoulder and blew me a kiss.

"I did my chores and ate the dinner that mama had left for me and fell asleep on the floor in front of the fireplace. I woke up and went to the barn and pulled the lambs. Everything went fine, until the second night. That's when I got scared.

"A big storm came up and it was blowing and raining, and I didn't know whether to be scared for the sheep or myself or wondering if mama and daddy got caught in the storm on their way home. I was worried for my mama and the more I sat there and thought about her and a tiny baby being caught out in that storm, the more upset I got. I really didn't care if my daddy came back, but I was scared for mama. I cried myself to sleep laying on the floor in front of the fireplace that night. As far as I can remember, that was the last time in my life that I cried."

"Mr. Carr, I have a hard time believing that the last time you ever cried was when you were six years old. Certainly, something has made you sad since then."

"Lots of things have made me sad, Padre. I've just chosen not to cry about them. It doesn't do any damn good anyway."

"So, your parents made it home safely with your twin brothers? And the sheep survived the storm?"

"Oh, hell yes. Everything turned out fine, except daddy now had two more mouths to feed. Daddy's alcohol consumption increased, but the amount of food on the table didn't.

"Listen Padre, all this damn talking is wearing me out. I think I'm going to nap for a while."

"Well Mr. Carr, I'll let you get some rest, but I'm looking forward to hearing more of your stories."

"Well, you come back again tomorrow, and I'll dazzle you with some more bullshit. I'm not sure why you want to hear this crap anyway. Our family wasn't anything special. There were dirt poor farmers all over Iowa back in those days."

"I'm sure that's true Mr. Carr, but this is your story, and I want to hear it."

XIII

"Well good morning, Padre. Looks like it's a nice day outside," said Dan looking out the window.

"Mr. Carr, it is a wonderful day outside. The sun is shining, the birds are chirping, and the sun was warm on my face as I walked in."

"Well, what in the hell are you doing in here? You should be sitting by a pond somewhere; catching bass and drinking beer."

"That does sound nice Mr. Carr, but you have a story to tell me."

"Un-freaking-believable! I can promise you that I wouldn't spend a day like today sitting in a sterile hospital room listening to you tell me about your childhood."

"Well why don't we go outside and talk."

"Padre, in case you haven't noticed, my legs don't work so well."

"We can get a wheelchair Mr. Carr."

"I don't know Padre, but that sun does look pretty nice."

"It is Mr. Carr! It's a beautiful day that God has given us."

"You know, if you get me outside, I might not come back in?"

"That's a chance I'm willing to take Mr. Carr. I'll go to the nurse's station and get a wheelchair."

Fr. Viloria returned from the nurse's station with a wheelchair and a nurse's aide to lift Mr. Carr into the chair. The aide got him positioned in the chair and put a blanket over his lap. Fr. Viloria thanked the aide and wheeled Mr. Carr toward the elevator.

They exited the West side of the building and headed South down the sidewalk toward a courtyard. Fr. Viloria parked the chair in direct sunlight and Mr. Carr tilted his head back, soaking up the rays and a slight smile emerged on his face.

"Hey Padre? You don't happen to have a cigarette, do you?"

"No, Mr. Carr. I don't smoke and this is a tobacco free hospital."

"Tobacco free huh? They have drugs inside this hospital that would stone the devil himself, but they won't allow a simple cigarette. I've never understood bureaucracies, but I guess 'Tobacco Free' looks good on a sign."

"This is a place of healing Mr. Carr. Cigarettes are known to cause disease. This hospital does everything they can to prevent and treat disease."

"And keep people alive against their wishes. Don't forget that, Padre."

"Okay Mr. Carr. We've had this discussion before. Last time we talked you were telling me about when your parents brought your twin brothers home from the hospital."

"Oh yeah. Well, our 50-acre farm could barely feed three people and as soon as the boys were weaned off of mama and started eating table food, we sure as hell didn't have enough for five mouths, so the portion sizes just kept getting smaller and smaller.

"I'd take my gun down to the draw and shoot rabbits and squirrels and bring them home and mama would cook them up, but have you ever tried to split a squirrel five ways for dinner Padre?"

"No, Mr. Carr, I can't say that I have."

"Well, it doesn't go far and our whole family was malnourished and sickly and of course daddy didn't spend any less on alcohol. If anything, he spent more to try and forget about how poor we were.

"In any event, I guess mama finally had enough of it and just up and walked away one day."

"What do you mean? Up and walked away?"

"Well, I was about 10 or 11 and my brothers would have been four or five. It was 1956 or 57. I'd been down in the draw hunting and mama was in the yard hanging clothes on the line. I'm not real sure where daddy was, but the boys were playing somewhere in the barn.

"I'd shot three or four squirrels and was walking across the field toward the house. I yelled out to mama, '*I got us some squirrels for dinner.*' She looked at me and smiled. My mama was beautiful. She usually wore her hair in a bun and always wore a dress, one that she had made herself. I don't ever recall her wearing makeup, but God Damn she was a looker! As a boy, I was in love with her.

Anyway, I got to the yard with them squirrels and she asked me to take 'em inside and put 'em in the sink and she'd get 'em cleaned up.

"So, I took the squirrels inside and put my gun away. I couldn't have been in there more than a few minutes. When I came back out, I saw my mama walking down the lane and over the hill and she had her hair down, like she did at night. I wasn't sure where she was going, but I wasn't too worried about it. I went and found my brothers in the barn and played with them for a few hours until we heard daddy's old truck coming up the drive. He'd finally bought a truck the year or two before. It was new to us, but it was all beat to hell. Between alcohol and parts for that truck, Daddy spent just about all the money he made. But, anyway, my brothers and me, we were all thinking about the squirrel that mama was cooking up for dinner and ran to the house.

"We got to the house at the same time as daddy and I ran in expecting to smell fried squirrel and potatoes and white gravy. But the squirrels were laying in the sink, just like I left 'em."

"Where the hell is your mama?" said Daddy

"I don't know. I saw her walking down the lane earlier today. I'm not sure where she was going."

"And you just let her walk away? Did you get all your chores done? Who the hell's going to cook this dinner?"

I didn't know which question to answer first, and I didn't know what was going on. I didn't know where my mama went, and I didn't have answers for daddy.

"Yes sir, I got all my chores done. I can cook the squirrel. I know how."

"I'm gonna go look for your mama. I'll be back in a little while to eat."

"Yes sir."

XIV

"Wow, that's quite a story Mr. Carr. So, what happened to your mother?"

"I don't know Padre. Never saw her again. She just up and walked away and abandoned us. I don't know if it was me, or the twins or Daddy, but something was too much for her and she couldn't handle it anymore.

"I suppose she could have went off and killed herself, but you'd think someone would eventually find a body. No one ever said that they saw her, not walking, not riding a bus, nothing. I was the last one to ever see her. The last time I ever saw my mama she was walking away, over the hill; still wearing her apron, but with her hair down, like she did when she went to bed. She was so beautiful. I like to think she went to Hollywood and became a famous actress or to New York to become a rich businessman's wife. At least that's what I tell myself."

"Mr. Carr, that had to be traumatic for a 10- or 11-year-old boy."

"You know Padre, it probably would have been if that was the end of it. But I didn't even have time to comprehend what had happened. The next morning Daddy said he had to go into town for something. I decided that I better show my brothers what I knew about shooting and cleaning and cooking wild game just in case mama never came back. I knew I didn't want to be the one responsible for cleaning and cooking, so I figured I'd show them what I knew.

"We spent the morning down in the draw trying to shoot a squirrel that they could practice on. We hadn't had any luck when we heard Daddy's truck coming up the lane. We headed back to the house, hoping he found mama in town."

"Boys! Come on in the house." He yelled to us as we came across the field.

"I can't remember ever seeing Daddy that sober. I hadn't seen his eyes that clear in years and there wasn't a trace of liquor on his breath.

"Boys, I'm not sure what's happened to your mama, but I need to go look for her. There's a good chance that she's sick in the head and she could just be out wandering or she coulda' jumped on a train or she could be laying in a holler somewhere. I just don't know.

"But I'm gonna go find her and I don't know how long it will take. I don't expect Danny to run the house and farm all by himself while I'm gone. All three of you boys are going to go live with the McClintic's, down the road, until I get back. Gather up your things and get in the truck."

"We each had a few odds and ends that we'd accumulated over the years that were special to us; deer antlers and turtle shells and turkey feathers and shiny rocks and what not. We each threw our 'valuables' in a sack with a change of clothes and jumped in the back of the truck.

"The McClintic's lived about four miles from our farm. They were an older couple whose kids had grown and moved away. Mr. McClintic had a bad knee and had a hard time getting around. We pulled up in front of their house and daddy told us to stay put for a few minutes while he went inside.

"About that time, I saw a baby bird near the side of the house that had fallen out of its nest and was struggling in the grass. It was flapping with everything it had, but it wasn't going anywhere. The McClintic's cat was stalking it from a few yards away and I wanted to save that baby bird.

"I jumped out of the bed of the truck and went and picked it up. I was walking toward the back of the house to find a safe spot to set him down when I walked past an open window and heard my Daddy and Mr. McClintic talking."

"Like I said Roy, I have no idea where my wife is and it's highly unlikely that I'll ever find her. As far as I'm concerned, she doesn't want to be found and she's never coming back. I've already notified Mr. Scott that I'm breaking the lease on the farm, and I have no intention of ever coming back either.

"I know you need some help around here since your boys are all grown and you've got a bum leg. My oldest boy is in sixth grade, but he's had enough school. He'll quit school and work here on the farm for you if you can make sure that the twins get a high school education. They're not much help yet but give them a few years and they'll be able to earn their keep too.

"I just can't head West and ever hope to make anything of myself with three boys in tow. I hope you understand, and I hope you'll take me up on my offer."

"I didn't know what to think Padre. First my Mama and then my Daddy, just abandoning me. That'll mess with a kid's head, you know. I know I wasn't much of a student, but my Daddy gave me away to ensure that my brothers got an education. Do you have any idea what that feels like to a kid, Padre?"

"No, Mr. Carr. I honestly can't imagine what that feels like. And I don't suppose that most people can."

"Well, Daddy came out of the house and repeated the lie about going to look for Mama and that he'd be back when he found her. I'm pretty sure that was the day my wall went up Padre and it's never come back down. My Daddy hugged all three of us and he looked me in the eye, and I could see tears in his eyes. I know he was sad and I probably shoulda' been, but I knew he was lying to us, and he wasn't coming back.

"I didn't hug him back. I didn't smile and I didn't shed a tear. I just stared at him, like a full-grown man who's been cheated. My face was a stone. I don't know if he knew that I knew the truth, but the last time my Daddy saw me I made sure that he knew I was disgusted with him."

"Mr. Carr, that is horrible. I can't imagine the pain and betrayal you must have felt."

"Yeah, well, let me tell you Padre. That was the beginning of the end for me. The McClintic's put my brothers up in a room in the house. They made a place for me to sleep in a somewhat finished portion of the barn. I was definitely slave labor, and they treated me like it. It wasn't long before my own brothers forgot that we were blood. They tried to order me around just like Mr. McClintic. Of course, I never listened to them, but it was just the idea that they thought they were part of a family, and I was just an unpaid, hired hand.

"Padre, I think I've had enough of the sunshine for today. I think I need a nap."

"Yes Mr. Carr. I suppose you do. Perhaps we can talk again tomorrow?"

"Possibly."

XV

"Good morning, Mr. Carr. How are you today?"

"What the hell is so good about it, Padre?", said Mr. Carr as he looked out the window without expression.

"Well, Mr. Carr, it is another beautiful day. Another opportunity to do the Lord's work. Shall we go outside and feel the sunshine and you can tell me more about your life?"

"No, not today."

"Mr. Carr, did you have a bad night? Did you not sleep well?"

"Did you sleep well, Padre?"

"Honestly, Mr. Carr, I woke in the middle of the night, thinking about you. Thinking about how you were robbed of your childhood. Thinking about how both of your parents abandoned you. Thinking about how your brothers were cared for and you were made to sleep in the barn and drop out of school in the sixth grade. So, no, I guess I didn't really sleep well."

"Imagine doing that for 60 years, Padre. It wears a man out."

"I'm sure it does Mr. Carr, but you told me before about Malaya, the mother of your first child. You told me that being with her was the last time you were truly happy."

"Yeah, what about it?"

"How did you get to know her?"

"Ah, shit. Padre, I just don't think I can do this. Not today anyway. Look, I'm a grumpy, old bastard who just wants to die and I have no problem being a pain in the ass to everyone in this joint. But, for some reason, I don't feel like being a prick to you."

"Mr. Carr, I'm not sure I understand what you're saying."

"Padre, get the hell out of my room. Do you understand that? Come back tomorrow and maybe I'll be less of an asshole. But don't count on it."

"Ok Mr. Carr. I'll leave you be. But I have the next two days off and I'm going to visit my sister. I won't see you again until Wednesday."

"Well, with any luck, I'll be dead by Wednesday."

"That's not likely Mr. Carr, and if it were true then it would certainly be devastating."

"Devastating? How so?"

"You're not yet ready to meet the Lord Mr. Carr. And, while I pray for you daily, I've not heard your entire story. Without knowing your entire story, I can't adequately prepare you for your journey."

"Padre, it's a real noble profession that you've chosen, and I sincerely appreciate the effort that you're making, but honestly, the only thing you can do to help me prepare is pick out a handbasket, 'cause I'm going to hell."

"And what makes you think that Mr. Carr?"

"Because I've lived a shitty, selfish, worthless life, Padre. I haven't opened a bible in over 60 years, but my mama read it to me enough when I was a kid to know that I've committed every one of the seven deadly sins; quite frequently."

"But, Mr. Carr, our Lord is a forgiving Lord. We need only ask forgiveness and it will be granted. Perhaps the reason you were unsuccessful in your suicide attempt is that you were given an opportunity to repent, to be able to enter Paradise."

"Padre, I'm not completely sure that I believe in heaven and hell. Sometimes I think that the lights just go out and that's the end. But, if there's a heaven, then I know without a doubt that Malaya is either already there or she will be someday.

"I'm going to die sometime in the next few weeks. I have nothing better to do during the rest of my time than talk to you. If talking to you could possibly result in me seeing Malaya again someday, then I guess I have nothing else to lose.

"Go visit your sister and when you get back on Wednesday, I'll continue my story."

"Do you promise?"

"Yep."

"Do you promise that you won't give the nurses a hard time while I'm gone?"

"Hell no, I'm not going to promise that. Now get the hell out of my room."

A slight smile appeared on Fr. Viloria as he turned to leave the room. Dan Carr looked back toward the window and a hint of a grin formed at the corners of his mouth. Wednesday was a long, two days away.

XVI

"Mr. Carr? Mr. Carr?" Fr. Viloria was afraid that during his absence Mr. Carr had actually passed away. After all, he was very pale and sickly looking in his hospital gown.

But he saw his chest rise and fall. He wasn't dead yet. Fr. Viloria had to get the rest of the story. He had to know what made Dan Carr's life so miserable. He had to have something to pray about. He had to save this man's soul.

"Mr. Carr? It's me, Fr. Viloria."

"Good morning, Padre."

Finally, Mr. Carr answered, and Fr. Viloria sighed in relief.

"Mr. Carr, it is a beautiful spring day. Perhaps you would like to venture outside?"

"You know what Padre? I don't care if we go out or stay in, I have a hell of a story to tell you."

"Really? Well, if it's all the same to you, Mr. Carr, I would prefer to hear it outside, in the sunshine."

"Padre, I've had some time to do some thinking about things. You know about how I got here. It's been a pretty shitty ride. If I tell you all about the ride, and you still think that you can get me to heaven; to see Malaya, then I'll tell you all about it. I'll tell you all about the blood and guts, the drugs and booze, the sins; and then I'll tell you about the really bad shit."

"Mr. Carr, right now there is nothing I want to hear more than your story. Your story belongs to you. I'll never hear another like it. My job right now is to get you to heaven. That requires me to hear your story; no matter what."

"Well, Padre. Get a son-of-a-bitch in here to put some clothes on me and we'll go outside."

XVII

Fr. Viloria pushed Mr. Carr's wheelchair down the ramp and through the gardens; past the spot where they had sat and talked just a few days ago. He made his way across gravel, mulch and through the woods, towards the banks of the small creek that bordered the hospital property.

"Mr. Carr, this is as far as I can legally take you. This is the boundary of the hospital property."

"Padre, this view is perfect. Now, where were we?"

"Well, Mr. Carr; the last time we really talked, you were telling me about your father giving you and your brothers to the neighbor family and you were treated like slave labor, while your brothers were welcomed into the family. Does that sound about right?"

"Yeah, that sounds about right. So, I was 11 or 12 years old, and my twin brothers were about 5 or 6. It didn't take long before they forgot I was their brother. I was just a hired hand, and they could order me around.

"I tried several times to talk to them about the situation and remind them that we were blood, but it went in one ear and out the other. They were just too young to understand.

"After about a year I'm pretty sure they forgot mama and daddy and the fact that I was their brother."

“Mr. Carr! That’s horrible. Your own flesh and blood, forgetting that you’re related.”

“Padre. You’ll get much more out of this if you just listen. You don’t need to remind me about how horrible it was. I know you’re trying to sympathize with me but just listen; and you’ll have a better chance of getting me to heaven.”

“Yes, of course, Mr. Carr. Please continue.”

“Well, as luck would have it, I hit a growth spurt during my thirteenth year. I shot up to nearly six foot before I was 14. My mind may have been warped, but I was the size of a full-grown man.

“Pretty soon the seed dealer and hardware store in town thought I was my own man. They would mistake me for a sharecropper and ask which farm I was working. They were trying to extend me credit, like I was a contract holder.

“At first, I didn’t know what to make of it. I lay awake in the barn at night wondering if I could get my own 40 acres and be my own man. I was only 14 years old, and I was being extended credit in town. Do you understand what I’m talking about Padre?”

“Not entirely Mr. Carr. But keep going, I think you are educating me as the story progresses.”

“Well, I could have gone and found a job sharecropping just about anywhere, but my situation wouldn’t have improved much. Sharecropping would have paid just enough for a roof and some food, which is what the McClintic’s were giving me for working on their farm. Plus, I would have had the added burden of bringing in a crop, or I would be responsible for the cost of the seed and planting.

“Now, being extended credit for seed and hardware is one thing, but a loan to purchase property; an opportunity to truly be my own man, that required a loan at the bank. So, one day I strolled into the bank and decided that I would try to take out a loan to purchase the Schmidt farm a few miles away. I’d heard Mr. McClintic talking about the fact that the 50 acres were for sale. It was 38 acres tillable, and 12 acres wooded. It would have been an ideal place for a young farmer to get his feet wet and establish himself."

"At 14 years old you tried to get a loan to buy 50 acres. Wow, that's quite an undertaking."

"Well, it turned out to be more of an undertaking than my young brain had imagined it would be. The bank needed some documentation. They wanted a birth certificate or drivers' license or something that identified who I was. I didn't have any of that. As far as the State of Iowa was concerned, I didn't even exist. I was born at home, so I had no birth certificate. I wasn't legally old enough to drive so I had no drivers' license. I'd attended the Deer Creek country school, but I have no idea whether or not they kept any records at all. For the most part, I was a ghost.

"I walked out of the bank that day and decided that I was done being an unpaid hired hand. Supposedly, I was working for Mr. McClintic to put my brothers through high school, but they had forgotten that I was their brother, so I was done with that shit. It was already late summer and with winter coming on I didn't intend to spend another cold spell in that barn. I was going to head south."

"Unbelievable Mr. Carr. At 14 years old you were just going to hit the road and find a way to make it on your own. That is truly remarkable."

"Well, if I had turned into the next Sam Walton then it might have been remarkable Padre, but I can't really say that I had a head for business or much of a moral compass and I was just trying to survive.

"I did, however, make it to Galveston, Texas before Christmas of that year, which would have been 1960. I hitched a few rides, jumped a few trains and did a lot of walking, but that 1,000-mile trip was a blessing to me. I did a hell of a lot of growing up between September and December of that year."

“How do you mean Mr. Carr? You were already on your own and you have stated that you were nearly six feet tall and mistaken for a full-grown man in your home community.”

“Well, Padre. There’s just something about being on your own and responsible for your own survival that makes a man out of you. I don’t know that I can explain it. It could have something to do with getting jumped and beaten. It could have something to do with the whores on the rail line, or maybe a meal from a dumpster after a week of nothing, but something about that journey made me feel like less of a boy and more of a man.”

“I think I will never fully relate, but I can start to understand Mr. Carr. So, how was your first Christmas in Galveston?”

“Well, the entire reason I ended up there was due to a prostitute I met in Tulsa. She told me that she had a sister in a place called Galveston, which I had never heard of. Of course, I had never heard of Tulsa before the train I was on rolled into town. Her sister had written to her and told her that the military bases in Galveston had decreased quite a bit following World War II, and the area was left with a shortage of strong, young men. I figured that I was one of those and I should be able to pretty easily find a job.

“I arrived in Galveston and headed to the busiest tavern I could find. On my journey I’d learned that that is where business is conducted and if someone is looking for labor that’s where they look. I hadn’t been inside 15 minutes and I was getting looks and whispers about who I was. Apparently, Galveston was a small town and everyone in this particular tavern knew one another.

“Remember Padre, I was only 14 years old at the time. I bellied up to the bar and asked for a shot of whiskey, which I had become accustomed to on my trek. The bartender, being wary of outsiders, asked me to put some money on the bar before he would pour. I had money, some of which I had stolen or swindled and some of which I’d earned doing various odd jobs along my journey and I put some on the counter and he poured.

"Four or five shots later I noticed a man getting gradually closer to me on my left. He was a rather small man and was sharply dressed. I kept glancing at him from the corner of my eye, which was becoming quickly blurred from the whiskey.

"Finally, I turned to the well-dressed man and asked if I could help him with something."

He said, "*Yes, in fact you can, if you're interested in making some money.*

"Money was music to my ears, and I maybe should have tried to negotiate a little, but I didn't know any better and I was starving and homeless and I didn't know a soul in town and this man offered me work, so I was interested. He told me to report to the docks at 6:00 am the next morning. I slept with the bums in the rail yard that night and for some reason thought it would be the last night I would ever be homeless. I was going to be a working man the next day.

"I showed up at the docks a little before 6:00 am, just like he asked. I didn't know the guy's name, so I didn't know who to ask for. I just kind of loitered around until someone asked me if I was lost. I told them that a short man in a nice suit offered me a job the night before and told me to be here in the morning. The guy pointed toward a faded yellow, cinder block building about a quarter mile away."

"I think the man you're looking for is in there." He said.

"I strolled the length of the dock; feeling very much out of place and very unsure what I was getting myself into. I finally entered the cinder block building and the man from the night before was looking through some paperwork on his desk.

"You're late! You can't expect a full day's pay if you don't do a full day's work! This job pays $7 a day and you just got docked a quarter. From now on, work starts at 6:00 am. Head back down to the other end of the dock and ask for Jake. Tell him you're the new guy."

"I thought about protesting being docked a portion of my pay, and then I thought about telling him to kiss my ass and just walk away. But I'd drank half of the $8 I had to my name the night before and I needed the money. I walked back to the other end of the dock and asked for Jake. Jake turned out to be the same guy who pointed me in the direction of the cinder block building.

"Jake sent me further on down the dock to look for a guy named Mike. Mike would be my boss and father figure for the next year of my life. Mike gave me a hard hat and a pair of leather gloves. Dock work was hard, dirty and dangerous. There were lots of guys working on the docks with missing fingers and hands, permanent limps to their walk and bad backs. As the new guy, I got the worst of the worst.

"We mainly unloaded and reloaded cargo ships. Most of the work was done by the older guys running the forklifts and cranes, but some of it had to be done by hand. I have no idea how many hours I worked that first day, but it was well after dark when I emerged from the belly of a ship, covered head to toe in dirt and walked back down to the yellow, cinder block building.

"Doing odd jobs on my journey from Iowa to Texas was the first time in my life that I had ever been paid to work. I would help a farmer put up a fence, or help a mechanic rotate tires or change oil; just whatever I could find in the town I was passing through. I always made it known that I was just passing through and whoever I was working for would pay me in cash at the end of the day. So, I walked into the cinderblock building expecting to get $6.75 at the end of my first day.

"What the hell do you want? Was it too much work? Are you letting me know you won't be back tomorrow?" said the little man in the nice suit.

"No, I'll be back. I just came to collect my pay."

"Let me explain something to you, Son. You get paid once a week around here, on Friday afternoon. Today is only Tuesday. If

you don't show up every day for the rest of the week, you won't get paid a dime. Now get the hell out of my office. I shouldn't need to see you again until Friday." He said.

"I had planned on finding a cheap room to rent that night. I'd been looking forward to a hot bath and hot meal all day long. The $4 I had in my pocket would get me a gourmet meal, but it also had to last me the rest of the week. I figured I could handle three more nights at the rail yard with the bums until I got paid on Friday. I could manage to eat for $1 a day, so I was all set.

"I worked the rest of the week and smelled pretty bad by the time work ended on Friday. I was also starving. The whistle blew that told us to quit work for the day and by the time I got out of the container I was working in, there was a long line of guys outside the yellow building. I figured they must be lined up to get paid and I found myself a spot in the line.

"The line of men was moving in one door of the yellow building and exiting on the other side. Each of the guys coming out had an envelope in his hand. When it was my turn, I followed the line inside and saw the small man in the suit sitting behind his desk. There was a stack of envelopes on it. He would look through the stack, find the worker's name and hand him the envelope. The small man only looked up long enough to see who was next in line. No words were exchanged.

"When it came my turn, he glanced up and saw it was me. Instead of looking through the envelopes on the desk, he opened the drawer and got one out and handed it to me. Still no words exchanged. I walked out with plans to go straight to a boarding house for a soft bed, hot bath and big meal. As I walked, I opened my envelope. I counted the ones and the change and then stopped walking. I took it out and counted it again. There was a mistake. I turned to go back to the building, but my boss, Mike, had been watching me and he caught me before I could go back in."

"Hey, new guy, what's up?" said Mike.

"There's money missing from my envelope. I think there's been a mistake. I worked four full days this week, minus the 25 cents that he said he was going to dock me on my first day. It's short."

"I think it would be a bad idea if you went back in there. Let me take a look at what you have."

"I handed the envelope to Mike, and he counted the money."

"How much do you think you should have gotten paid?"

"I was told the job pays $7 a day. I guess I was late on Tuesday, so I got docked a quarter. I was on time the other three days, so I should get $27.75, but there's only $21.75."

"What's your name, new guy?"

"Dan."

"Dan, let's don't stand here in the dark and cold. Come with me to the bar and I'll buy you a beer and explain what's going on."

"So, I went with Mike, the only person in Galveston who had offered me anything; except for the small man in the suit, who offered me a job and then screwed me over."

XVIII

"Mr. Carr, said Fr. Viloria. "I am always astounded by your life story. It is so different from my life and on the one hand I just can't relate, but your story telling is so detailed, that I can certainly relate to you as a human."

"Well Padre, replied Dan. "I would certainly hope that no one could relate to my life story. I haven't even gotten to the bad part yet. It's really just a story about where I come from and, I guess, how that shaped who I became; a bitter, angry, old man, who just wants to die."

"Certainly Mr. Carr. All of our life experiences help shape who we become, the good and the bad. I would love to keep listening, if you are in the mood to keep talking."

"We're here and I've got nothing better to do. Besides, I'm not sure how much longer I'm going to be around. You better take advantage of listening now, while I can still talk.

"So, I was just leaving the docks with my first paycheck to go get a beer with my boss, Mike. We walked a short distance to the same bar where I was first offered the job. It was crowded with guys whose names I didn't know, but I saw daily at work. Mike walked to a table in the back, and I followed. There really wasn't a place in the bar to have a quiet conversation, but the table in the back was as good as it was going to get."

"Have a seat Dan. I'm going to get us a drink."

"I took the chair with my back to the wall, so I could keep an eye on the crowd. Mike came back with a beer and a shot for each of us."

"Listen Dan, I don't know how much you understand about this organization, or the pecking order, or what's expected of you, but you seem like a good kid and a hard worker. I don't want to see anything bad happen to you. There's money to be made working here, you just have to stick with it."

"Mike, I'm pretty sure I know what's expected of me. I do the shit work that you tell me to do. Beyond that, I don't know what you're talking about with this organization and pecking order stuff. Hell, about the only thing I know, other than that I do the shit work, is that your name is Mike and the guy who walks around with the clipboard is Jake. I don't even know who the man in the yellow building is or what company I work for!"

"Ok, Dan, let's start at the beginning. How old are you?"

"Old enough."

"Ok, that's fair. Where are you from?"

"North of here. Quite a ways north."

"How did you end up in Galveston?"

"I mostly walked. Hopped a few trains now and then."

"Good, those are all the right answers, at least for now. Don't try to make too many friends and don't tell anyone too much about yourself. Just come to work each day and do your shitty work. Things will get better.

"As far as the organization, right now, you and I work for two different companies. The man in the yellow building is Mr. Elkhart. He owns the company, and you work for him.

"I work for the International Longshoremen's Association Local 20. We're the union that does the work on the Galveston docks. Jake is my boss and our organization does most, but not all of the work associated with loading and unloading cargo for Mr. Elkhart's company. He doesn't really like us, but he doesn't have a choice. We're good at what we do, and we make him a lot of money. Even though we don't work for him, he's still the one who pays us each individually. If he tries to screw one of us over, the rest of us will make sure that his docks don't operate until he makes it right. He doesn't like disruptions, so he usually doesn't try to screw us over."

"I don't understand. If Mr. Elkhart doesn't like you guys, why doesn't he just hire his own people?"

"Technically, we are his people, but our loyalty is with the union, not Mr. Elkhart. You have to go back about 40 years to understand how it all came about, but let's just say that working conditions on the docks used to be horrible, as opposed to just shitty, like they are now. The workers had enough and went on strike in 1920. They negotiated better pay, safer working conditions, a whole host of concerns that improved the workday, but cost the company more money. They really haven't liked us much since then, but they tolerate us, because, like I said, we're good at what we do, and we police ourselves."

"So, why don't I work for the union? Why do I work for Mr. Elkhart?"

"There are a few low-level jobs that are considered to be non-skilled. These aren't part of the union. Mr. Elkhart can hire whoever he wants and pay them whatever he wants. He expects us to supervise you, but in all honesty, you're really on your own.

"Now, this is where things can work out for you, if you play your cards right. Eventually, people in the union will retire, or get hurt and can't come back to work and will have to be replaced. The union can replace our members with whoever we want, but the last five replacements have come from the ranks of Mr. Elkhart's hired

labor. That's actually how you got offered your job. Ed had been a laborer for about four months when Max broke his back, and we needed a replacement. We all saw Ed at work every day, sort of knew who he was, and made him an offer to join the union. He's making $2.25 an hour now, compared to your $7.00 a day."

"About that $7.00 a day. I guess Mr. Elkhart has the right to screw me over since I'm not protected by the union?"

"Well, he could screw you over, but I don't think that's what happened here. Elkhart is an asshole and a greedy bastard, but generally he's fair. How much did you say you thought you were supposed to make?"

"$7.00 a day for four days, minus $0.25 because he said I was late my first day. It should have been $27.75."

"Do you remember the hard hat that you were given on the first day? And the gloves? Well, Mr. Elkhart can charge you for those. $2.50 for the hat and $1.00 for the gloves. Don't worry, it's only a one-time deal."

"That still leaves me short by $2.50."

"Well Dan, here's the part that you're not going to like. The union dues are $2.50 a week."

"Union dues? What the hell does that mean? You said I'm not in the union."

"Correct, but you're eligible to join the union when there's an opening, so you go ahead and pay your dues now. I promise, it will all be worth it."

"A decent room in this town costs $4.00 a day and one, good, hot meal a day is $1.25. Even without union dues, I'd be struggling to make it."

"Yeah, if I were you, I'd skip the decent room and spend my

money on food and a good bottle of whisky each week. And look on the bright side, Mr. Elkhart may not be paying you minimum wage, but he is paying you in cash, so you don't have to pay taxes."

"Minimum wage? Taxes? What's that? Another one of those great union deals that I have to pay for but don't get?"

"Don't worry about it for right now. Listen, I've got an extra room in the back of my garage. I'll rent it to you for $6.00 a week. It doesn't have any plumbing, but it does have a kerosene heater. That should save you enough money that you can check into a motel on the weekend and get a shower and a shave."

"Thanks Mike, I'll think about it. I need to figure out if this is where I need to be right now, or if I should just keep moving."

"Well, it's there if you want it. I'll get us one more beer, then I'm heading home for the night."

"I stayed in the rail yard again that weekend. It got pretty cold a few nights. I thought about having a room to myself, even if it was only in the back of a garage, at least it would have heat and hopefully a mattress.

"I showed up to work on Monday and when the whistle blew, I found Mike."

"Hey, Mike, I've got your $6.00. I'll take the room for the week."

"Dan, you do realize that this is Christmas Eve, right?"

"No, it didn't really occur to me."

"Well, we don't work tomorrow, and I have a family gathering to attend tonight."

"Oh, okay. I didn't know we didn't work tomorrow. I was kind of counting on a full week's pay."

"I tell you what Dan. As your Christmas gift, take your $6.00 and go get a motel room, a hot meal and a bottle of whiskey. Here's my address. Come by tomorrow, late afternoon, and I'll get you set up in the garage. I won't charge you rent for your first week."

"Are you sure?"

"I'm sure. I'll have you mow the yard or clean the gutters or something like that to make up for it."

"Padre, to this day, that is the most generous Christmas gift I ever received."

"Wow, Mr. Carr. It sounds like Mr. Mike was exactly what you needed in your life at that moment."

"Yeah, you could say that. Without him, I probably would have moved on from Galveston as I didn't really see how I was gonna make much of a life there. But, like most things in my life, meeting Mike only led to heartache later on."

"How do you mean Mr. Carr?"

"I think I need to rest Padre. Maybe we can talk more this evening."

"Sure. I'll take you back to your room."

XIX

It was early afternoon and Dan felt exhausted as the nurse's aide put him back in his bed. His body was certainly becoming weaker and his head hurt most of the time now due to the starvation. Every time he closed his eyes to rest; he hoped that this would be the time he never woke up.

Dan had a restless sleep. Each time he was able to dose off, visions of past demons crept into his thoughts. Visions of people he had done wrong in his life. Times he had cheated, stolen, squandered, been unfaithful, caused pain. Images flipped through his mind like a slideshow, each one reminding him of the worthlessness of his life and the path of destruction he had left.

Dan tossed and turned and was suddenly startled awake by one of the visions. It was his mother, walking away down the road, just like the last time he had ever seen her. She was beautiful, just like he remembered her. When he was ten or eleven years old, she just kept walking; but, in this vision, she turned around and looked at him and said something.

"What's that, mama? Wha'd you say?

And he was awake. His heart pounding. A cool bead of sweat on his brow. Dan felt nauseous, and for the first time since waking up in the hospital, he pressed the button to call the nurse.

The large, black man, who was a nurse's aide, entered his room and asked, "Yes, Mr. Carr, is there something I can help you with?”

Mr. Carr was having trouble breathing and he swallowed deep before he could reply, “Yeah. Can you call the Padre for me?”

XX

Fr. Viloria entered Dan's room.

"Mr. Carr, I came as soon as I could. I thought you would be sleeping for a while. What can I do for you?"

"Padre, I'm having nightmares, and I don't think I'm gonna be around much longer and I got things I need to tell you."

"Mr. Carr, the nightmares are most likely due to your brain not receiving any nutrients. As your body and your mind starve, your brain function will continue to deteriorate and play tricks on you. Perhaps you would be interested in something to eat?"

"NO! Dammit Padre, don't start with that shit again. I don't want to eat. I don't want to prolong my life a single minute longer than necessary. I need to continue my story."

"Very well Mr. Carr. It's still nice outside, would you like to go back out?

"No, just pull up a chair."

Fr. Viloria pulled the chair from the corner of the room to the head of Dan's bed and settled in.

"Mr. Carr, when you left off, it was Christmas. 1960 I believe."

"That's right. And my boss, Mike, had just given me a free

week of rent and suggested that I check into a motel for the night, so that's what I did. I also bought myself a bottle of whiskey and got drunk. I decided to skip the hot meal and had a half dozen chocolate moon pies with my whiskey. All-in-all, it was one of my better Christmases. The next afternoon, I walked to Mike's house and knocked on the door. Mike welcomed me in and introduced me to his wife, Bonnie.

"Welcome Dan, said Bonnie. I have a plate of food for you in the kitchen."

I looked at Mike, unsure if I should accept it.

"Go ahead," nodded Mike. "With winter finally here, you're going to need to fatten up a little bit."

"Padre, I followed her into the kitchen, and she pulled a foil wrapped plate of food out of the oven that had more food on it than I had ever seen at one time in my life. I'm talking about ham and potatoes and green beans and dinner rolls. She set it down on a little table in the kitchen and Mike and Bonnie talked while I ate until I was nearly sick. Then she got a pie out of the ice box and cut me a piece of it.

"While I stuffed myself, Mike explained to me that they had two sons who were both in the military and hadn't been able to come home for Christmas. Bonnie's family had come over for Christmas lunch and they had tons of leftover food. He said it would just go bad if I didn't eat it.

"I finished up my meal and dessert and thanked Bonnie at least a dozen times. Mike offered to show me to my room in the back of the garage. We entered through a side door and shimmied past his pickup truck, and he opened an interior door on the back wall. Once inside he pulled a small string on the ceiling and the room lit up."

"It's nothing fancy, but it's safe, dry and somewhat warm," said Mike.

"I looked around the small room. It was probably about eight foot by twenty foot. On one end there was a rollaway cot with a mattress and fresh linens, a side table with a lamp and an old easy chair. A set of empty shelves was built on the wall above the cot. At the other end was Mike's workbench and tools. It seems I probably wasn't the first person to rent this room from him.

"I thought about all the nights I had spent in the rail yards since running away and all the nights in the barn before that. Honestly, it was probably the nicest room I'd ever had up until that point in my life."

"I'll take it," I said to Mike.

"I figured you probably would. The missus also found some old clothes in the boys' room that she thought might fit you. They're not going to need them anymore and a change of clothes once or twice a week might feel pretty good."

"Yeah, I suppose you're right. Tell her I said thank you."

"Not a problem at all Dan. The shitters on the left out back, if you need that. The heater and matches are here and there's a stack of old books and magazines over there, if reading is your thing."

"Thank you, Mike. I think this is going to work out."

"Dan, I'm going to go back in and spend the rest of Christmas evening with my Bonnie. You can ride to work with me in the morning. Merry Christmas."

"Merry Christmas, I replied."

"So, things went on like that for a while. After the union dues were taken out of my weekly paycheck and I paid Mike his $6 a week, I had $26.50 left. I could go to the bar on Friday evening with the guys, check in to a motel for the weekend to get a hot shower, have a hot meal once a day and still have enough to save a little back each week.

"I couldn't read real well, but I liked looking through the old magazines. I especially liked the pictures in National Geographic. At night after work, I'd lay on my cot or sit in the chair and pretend that I was going to be a big game hunter in Africa, or a deep-sea fisherman in Alaska or an explorer in the South Pacific.

"I'd always come back from the motel on Sunday afternoon and have clean bed sheets and more often than not I'd be invited to join Mike and Bonnie for their Sunday evening dinner.

"I always offered to help out around the place and did quite a bit of lawn mowing, pulling weeds, helping to plant the garden in the spring, painted the garage in the summer; and even though I didn't expect it, sometimes there would be a couple dollars in an envelope on my freshly made bed on Sunday evening.

"Padre, I began to feel like maybe this is how real people lived. I was never hungry. I was never cold or wet while I slept. Mike and Bonnie certainly weren't family, but they treated me awfully good. I guess maybe with their boys off in the military, they missed having a kid around and used me to fill in. I sure didn't mind."

"No, I'm sure you didn't, Mr. Carr. It sounds like they were very good people."

"They were good people, Padre. But, like anything I ever came across that was good, it went to shit in a hurry.

"That next summer, probably around late August, both of the boys were able to come home on leave at the same time. Mark, the older son, was 21 and Mitch, the younger one, was 19. I had turned 15 sometime earlier in the Spring. The family sat out on the back patio every evening during the week and talked, and they invited me to join them for dinner each night.

"The boys were home for three weeks and on the first two weekends they had all kinds of family over for big meals. By the time the second weekend rolled around, even though I was invited to join them, I felt like I was suffocating under the weight of all the people. I decided I would get a motel room for the weekend and let them have their family time.

"I got back to the garage late on Sunday evening and I could hear Mike and his sons talking on the patio. They were laughing and drinking beer and telling stories about high school football games and being on patrol in some place called the demilitarized zone in South Korea. Padre, they had something I would never have, and it had been weighing on me all weekend. As good as I had it right then, I guess I was feeling pretty sorry for myself. They asked me to join them, but I said I was tired and just wanted to go to bed.

"I went to my little room in the back of the garage and found a plate of food waiting for me. I couldn't eat it. I didn't feel like looking at the magazines. I just went to bed. And I lay there thinking about how I didn't have any family. And I told myself that one day I would have a family like Mike and his Bonnie.

"I'd have a little house with a garage and a BBQ pit out back. I'd have a pickup truck and a few kids. I'd work hard every day and come home to a hot meal cooked by my wife. We'd have a Christmas tree and a Thanksgiving turkey.

"Padre, I was still pretty young, and I hadn't experienced much of the world at that point, but at the same time, I'd experienced enough to know that it wasn't gonna take much to make me feel complete. I drifted off to sleep thinking to myself that maybe everything was going to be just fine. Maybe I had life all figured out."

"Well, Mr. Carr. Having a happy family certainly goes a long way toward living a fulfilling life. Although you may have still been young, I'd say you did have quite a bit figured out."

XXI

"The boys left that Monday morning to go camp down the coast with some of their buddies from high school before they had to ship out the next weekend. I went back to work with a purpose other than just trying to survive. I caught myself daydreaming several times that day about having a little house and coming home from work to a wife and kids.

"During the nine or so months that I had worked on the docks, two of the union guys had retired and two of Mr. Elkhart's guys were hired to replace them. A few other of Mr. Elkhart's guys quit and I should have been next in line to move up. I just needed someone to retire or get hurt.

"Like I said, on that Monday, I'd been daydreaming off and on all day and for some reason I couldn't wait to get off work. Since his boys were gone camping, I thought maybe I could sit on the patio that night with Mike. I wanted to ask him how I could go about getting myself a pickup truck.

"I also knew that I had been doing a good job, and I was next in line to join the union, but it wasn't guaranteed. The union members had to vote to accept a new member. One of Mr. Elkhart's guys, Joe, had quit a few months earlier because he had been there the longest, but he wasn't asked to join the union. Another guy with less time had been asked ahead of him. So, I took every opportunity I could to do a little extra work and try to impress the union guys.

"It was getting late and was close to quitting time and we still had some freight to unload, and I had a container to clean before I could be done. It seemed like everyone had been moving in slow motion all day. Maybe it was the late summer heat, but the sun was going down and I just wanted to hurry up and get done.

"I came out of the container I had just finished cleaning and saw the last container of the day. The forklift was just sitting there, and no one was around. I thought I'd take it upon myself to get the freight unloaded so I could start cleaning. This would also show the guys that I was willing to jump in and help get the job done.

"Only the union guys were allowed to drive the forklift, but I'd seen it done thousands of times. There wasn't much to it. I jumped on and headed into the container. Lowered the forks and slid them under a stack of wooden crates. Raised the forks with the crates and started to back out.

"Everything was going great. I backed out of the container, thinking about how impressed the union guys would be when they saw me unloading and stacking freight for distribution. I knew exactly where the crates were supposed to go, and I was already planning on dropping them and coming back for another load.

"As I backed out of the container, I cut my wheels to the left in order to turn around and go drop the freight. But I still had the forks up too high, and the sudden turn caused the weight to shift."

Dan swallowed hard and his voice broke as he tried to continue the story.

"The forks were too high. I forgot to lower them when I turned. They were too high. Do you understand what I'm saying, Padre? The forklift wasn't made to turn like that with a heavy load up high. The load shifted and the weight of it pulled the forklift over."

Dan had tears welling up in his eyes. His voice cracked and the sound wouldn't come out.

"Mr. Carr, said Fr. Viloria, leaning forward in the chair and reaching out for Dan's arm. "Accidents happen. It was your first time driving the forklift. You were just trying to help. Just trying to impress the union guys. No one could fault you for trying to work hard."

"Fr., said Dan, fighting back the tears and trembling voice. "You don't understand. As I was backing out of the container, Mike came around the corner to see what was going on. I never saw him. I turned the wheels, and the weight shifted. The forklift turned over. I never saw him Fr. I didn't know he was there. The weight of the load shifted, and the forklift turned over and Mike was there. It all crashed down. The load, the forklift, me; everything crashed down, on top of Mike.

"I killed him."

XXII

Fr. Viloria was speechless. He couldn't remember the last time he was at a loss for words. Nothing seemed appropriate to say at the moment. He sat in stunned silence. Then thoughts began to flood his mind. Dan Carr had been so young and yet had experienced so much pain. A lifetime of pain for most people and he had only been 15 years old.

Fr. Viloria looked down at the 75-year-old man in the bed and wondered to himself how much more pain this man could describe to him. He had so far only talked about the first 15 years of his life. Fr. Viloria began to wonder if he was up to the task of making this man believe that Jesus could save his soul. Fr. Viloria still held tight to Dan's arm when he heard him speak again.

"I was hurt, but I wasn't injured. I had a few scrapes and bruises, but I jumped up off the tangled mess of forklift, splintered wooden crates, freight and mangled body. I didn't know yet who it was beneath the load, and I began trying to lift heavy crates and yelling for help. Men appeared from everywhere and started lifting and moving the crates. I could see that the forks of the lift were pressing across the abdomen of the lifeless body. The legs were extended into the opening of the cab, where I had just been sitting. The chest and head were buried in freight and debris.

"Someone yelled to call an ambulance and someone else sprinted toward the yellow building. The crates were loaded with tractor parts and weighed several hundred pounds each. A few of the crates had broken open and men were trying desperately to lift wooden crates, metal axles and the forklift itself. Another forklift was brought in to lift the one that was turned over. Everything had been cleared from the body and two of the guys pulled it out from under the overturned forklift. It was nearly dark by then and I still didn't know who it was or how bad he was. I had kind of been pushed aside when all of the help arrived.

"The looks on the faces of the men who pulled the body clear told me everything I needed to know about how bad he was. I stepped around the downed forklift and pushed through the crowd to try to find out who he was.

"Padre, said Dan, through exasperated breaths, "it may have been an accident, but I deserve to go to hell just for what I did to that man. I will never get the image of his crushed skull out of my mind. Bonnie couldn't even have an open casket at his funeral."

Dan's sobs were more pronounced now. His breaths were shallow and short. He tried to speak again but couldn't form the words.

"Mr. Carr, I'm pretty sure you should rest now. I think you've expended a lot of energy today. I'm going to talk to the nurse about getting you something to help you sleep."

Fr. Viloria left the room and Dan stared at the ceiling through teary eyes. God! Why couldn't he have killed himself? Why did he have to rehash all of the pain in his life? He just wanted to die. Why was it so damn hard to just die?

Fr. Viloria returned with the nurse. She found his porta-cath and inserted the end of a syringe.

"Mr. Carr, the nurse is going to give you something to help you sleep. Hopefully you can have a restful evening. I will be back first thing in the morning."

XXIII

Dan Carr did not sleep well that night. He never awoke, but his mind caused his body to toss and turn. His breathing became shallow, and he perspired all through the night.

The vision of his mother came back to him. She was walking away, down the road and over the hill, still in her apron, with her hair down. She turned to him and spoke.

"What is it mama? I can't hear you. Wait there. I'll come to you."

And then his dream would change to Mike's crushed skull and mangled body under the wreckage of the upturned forklift. Then back to Malaya on the beach of the South China Sea. They were having a picnic. Sitting under an umbrella. Dan reached in the basket for another roll and Malaya leaned in close to him.

"Dan, my darling, I'm pregnant."

Suddenly Dan saw his mother again, closer this time. She must be waiting for him on the road. His little 10-year-old legs can only carry him so quickly toward her. Her face looks old. Older than he remembers. And she has wrinkles that he never noticed before. She's still beautiful, even with streaks of gray in her long, flowing brunette hair. She smiles warmly as he approaches and reaches out her farm-worn, but motherly-soft hands.

In an instant, Dan is back on the docks. The chaos, the sirens, the yelling. Young Dan tried to scream, but nothing came out.

He had just killed a man. He was going to prison. He deserved to die. Dan backed away, gasping, trying to catch his breath. He was hyperventilating and seeing stars.

All night the images and flashbacks flickered in his mind. He wanted to talk to his mama. He wanted to tell Malaya how happy and excited he was for their baby and the life they would live back in the U.S. But mostly, he wanted to erase the image of Mike from his memory forever.

XXIV

Fr. Viloria stopped at the nurse's desk in the morning before going to Dan's room.

"How was everything last night with Mr. Carr?" he asked

"Honestly, Father, he slept through the night. Said the nurse as she flipped through his chart.

"It looks like his vitals were taken every hour and his heart rate was quite high, but in his condition, that's not necessarily something unexpected. He was wet with perspiration as well, but it looks like cool rags were applied. Again, not something unexpected for a man in the final stages of starvation."

"Nurse Kidwell, in your opinion, how long does he have left?"

"There's really no way of knowing. Tomorrow will be nearly two weeks since he has had any sort of nutrition. I wouldn't expect him to still be conscious a week from now. Once he slips into a coma, it really won't be long."

"Thank you, Nurse Kidwell," said Fr. Viloria as he walked down the hall toward Mr. Carr's room.

Fr. Viloria opened the door gently and peered inside. Mr. Carr appeared to still be asleep. He looked like a corpse lying in the bed. His skin was ashy and sunken in around his eyes and cheeks.

What remained of his thinning gray hair was rapidly disappearing. Fr. Viloria pushed the door a little wider and entered the room. He decided that he would sit next to Mr. Carr and pray until he woke up.

No sooner had Fr. Viloria pulled up a chair then Dan slowly turned his head in his direction. He tried to open his eyes, but they just rolled back into his head. As he opened his mouth to speak, what little saliva he had was gummy and stuck to his tongue and lips. A weak groan was the only sound he could make.

Fr. Viloria got a cup of water from the bedside table and dabbed a small sponge on the end of a stick around Dan's lips. Dan slowly licked his lips and swallowed, then opened his mouth for another few drops of water. After several swabs, Dan was finally able to clear his throat and form a few creaky words.

"Padre?" Dan whispered in a low growl

"Yes, Mr. Carr. I am here."

"Padre?" Said Dan just a little louder, but still rather gravelly

"Yes, Mr. Carr. It is me, Fr. Viloria. I am here. What can I do for you?"

"Padre, I would give anything for a shot of whiskey right now."

"Oh, Mr. Carr. It appears you might be feeling better?"

"No, not really. I could just use a shot."

"Well, Mr. Carr, you know that isn't something I can get for you. But there is something I feel that I urgently need to discuss with you."

"How about a little more of that water Padre? Then we can get on with chattin'."

“Certainly.” Said Fr. Viloria as he brought the cup of water with a straw to Mr. Carr’s mouth.

Dan sipped the rest of the cup of water in two big gulps.

“Well, that ought to get me through the day don’t ya think Padre?”

“It’s a good start Mr. Carr. Now, about what we need to discuss.”

“I thought you were just here to listen, Padre?”

“Yes, Mr. Carr. I am here to listen. That’s what I need to discuss with you. I feel it is urgent that I spend as much time as possible with you. Your time may be getting very short, and I want to make sure that you are fully prepared.

“The other bed in the room hasn’t been occupied since you’ve been here. I’ve brought my suitcase and I’m going to move in. That way whenever you are awake and feel like talking, I will be here to listen.”

“Well, Padre. I’m not in much of a position to throw you out, but I don’t think I’ll make for a good roommate. I’ve lived with a dozen different women in my life and none of them could stand me.”

“I’ll take my chances Mr. Carr. I do feel this is important.”

“Suit yourself, but don’t expect me to make your bed or fix your dinner; and since I have no intention of paying my half of the rent, you’re gonna have to pay all of it yourself.”

“Understood Mr. Carr, said Fr. Viloria with a grin. “Now, how was your night?”

“Awful. I kept having those bad dreams, only this time the nurse had me so drugged up that I couldn’t wake up to escape. I just tossed and turned and went from one bad dream to another.”

"I was afraid of that. I have prayed for you to find peace. I have prayed for you to find rest."

"I'm afraid that won't happen until I'm six feet under Padre."

"You may be right Mr. Carr, but you will find peace in heaven, and I will assure that you get there."

"Then I guess I better keep talking about my sins so you can make sure they're forgiven before I arrive. You don't have to remind me where we were Padre, I've still got the picture in my mind."

XXV

"As I was telling you yesterday, I saw Mike and I knew he was dead. I also knew that I killed him, and I was probably going to go to prison for it. I ran around the side of the container and bent over and puked my guts out. I stayed there for a minute or two, spitting the nasty bile out of my mouth and blowing my nose when I heard the ambulance arriving.

"It was dark, and the crowd had grown. Everyone was talking at once. I saw the headlights of the ambulance pull in at the other end of the dock near the yellow building and Mr. Elkhart came out and started walking our way, motioning for the ambulance to follow him.

"No one seemed to notice that I was standing there. No one seemed to know what happened. I thought for a moment that maybe no one knew it was me driving the forklift. Maybe no one knew that I killed Mike. But Mr. Elkhart was on his way, and he would get to the bottom of it. He would find out it was me and he would send me to prison for the rest of my life.

"So, I did the cowardly thing, and I ran. I ran from the docks and through the dark streets of Galveston. I made it as far as the bridge to the mainland and hid until traffic died down. I honestly thought that there would be a manhunt, and the causeway bridge would be closed. I was prepared to swim to the mainland if I had to. As the night wore on, I didn't notice any unusual activity on the bridge. I'm not sure how long I waited, but it was a few hours and traffic across the bridge had slowed to about one car every 10 or 15 minutes. The bridge is nearly two miles across and when the next car headed north, I took my chance and ran across the bridge behind it.

"One car passed me going south, but didn't even slow down. I made it to the mainland and just kept walking. I didn't know where I was going, but I avoided main roads and houses and skirted around the edge of Texas City. By the time the sun started to come up over my right shoulder, I had no idea where I was. I'd been walking on a gravel road and hadn't seen a car or truck for hours. I figured I was heading north, and I would just keep on heading that direction until the law caught up with me.

"Other than a few, I hadn't seen a soul since I ran from the docks, but just as the sun was peeking over the treetops, I saw a truck in the distance, heading toward me. I got off the road and into the woods. I was exhausted and needed a place to rest until night.

"I stayed in the woods and walked parallel to the gravel road for a distance. I could see a house up ahead and it had a large barn out back. I made my way around through the woods and into the barn and up to the hayloft. It seemed like a pretty good place to lay low and get some sort of plan together.

"Like I said, I had no idea where I was or where I was going. I thought that I had gone a good 15 or 20 miles from the docks, but I might have only gone 2 or 3. I realized that I only had a couple bucks in my pocket cause I hadn't planned on running away. I didn't own much, but everything I had was in the back of Mike's garage, especially my money. I'd been able to save nearly $200 during my time living at Mike's. I kept it all rolled up in a sock on the shelf where I kept my clothes.

"I'd been saving up to buy a truck. That's what I was going to talk to Mike about the night he died. It was more money than I had ever seen in one place at one time and sometimes I worried about it being in the garage, but I didn't know what else to do with it and I knew that Mike and Bonnie wouldn't take it, even if they happened to come across it.

"At the time, I certainly thought that money would come in handy for the journey I had ahead of me, especially since I had no idea where I was going. I thought all day about walking back to Mike's house once the sun went down, getting my money and then heading out again. I decided to nap for a while and then that was what I was going to do.

"I laid down in a haystack and was asleep in seconds. I probably could have slept for several days, but a truck pulling in woke me up. I crept around to where I could see through a gap in the barn siding and saw a man getting out of his truck. He was dusty and dirty, probably from a hard day's work. He could have been one of the dock workers, or a farm laborer or a factory guy. He was just a normal, regular, hard-working guy and I was a murdering coward hiding out in his barn.

"A woman came out the back door of the house with a baby on her hip. She gave the man a hug and a kiss and handed him the baby. He walked over toward the back of the house and sat down on a patio chair and bounced the baby on his knee while the woman walked to the back of the yard where the garden was and picked a few vegetables. She placed them in her apron and then went back inside. The man stood up with the baby and followed her in.

"They reminded me of Mike and Bonnie and what I wanted out of life. I sat back down and for the first time since the accident I thought about Mike's wife. I thought about his boys. I wondered how she reacted when she found out. I wondered about the boys on their camping trip down the island. Had they been informed? Would they still be heading back to Korea at the end of the week? How would Bonnie go on without him?

"You know Padre, these are the thoughts that go through a young man's head. I didn't have a clue how most of the world worked. I imagined Bonnie would become a lonely old widow working in a factory or taking in laundry, trying to keep the roof over her head. I imagined her boys being shipped back out to wherever they were going and missing their father's funeral. I think that was the most worthless I had ever felt in my life, Padre. If I had stuck a gun in my mouth that day, instead of 60 years later, I might have saved the world a whole shit-storm of trouble."

"Mr. Carr, you can't honestly believe that the last 60 years of your life have been lived for nothing. Whether you are part of their lives or not, you have children who wouldn't exist if it were not for you. Why don't you let me track them down and ask them if they would rather never been born?"

"I understand what you're trying to say, Padre. As far as my kids, they could be evil little bastards like me, or they could be doing quite well, considering they never had to deal with me as a father. I'm just trying to tell you that the few happy moments I've had in my life were followed immediately by tragedy and heartache of some sort. If I'd ended my life that day in 1961, I sure as hell wouldn't be laying here now rehashing all this shit and maybe God would have taken pity on my poor, ignorant, young soul. Back then I could have stood at the Pearly Gates and claimed ignorance and maybe he would have let me into heaven. Everything that's happened since then has been squarely on me."

"Our God is a very forgiving God, Mr. Carr. You'll be surprised how the weight will lift over the next few days.

"May I ask you Mr. Carr, did you return to Mike's house for your money?"

"No, I sure didn't."

XXVI

"I'll tell you exactly why I didn't go back for the money Padre. I figured I'd done enough damage to that family. Surely someone would have checked the garage looking for me after Mike was killed. They would have seen that I wasn't there and hadn't been there and all my stuff was just like I'd left it. Even if the law wasn't looking for me, which I was sure they were, I was too much of a coward to face Bonnie and the boys. I also thought it would have caused her a lot of pain if she found out I had snuck back in just to get some money, when her husband would be gone forever. I just couldn't bring myself to do it.

"I climbed down from the hayloft and walked around the edge of the property and past the garden. I took a few carrots, three or four tomatoes and a bell pepper. I made my way into the woods on the other side of the house and kept on walking. I walked all night, eating my vegetables as I went. By the time the sun came up the next morning I was close to another small town and needed a place to hide out and get some sleep. But there was something I had to do first.

"There was a general store at the edge of town. I was pretty sure that my picture would be on the front page of every paper in southern Texas, being wanted for murder and all, but I guess there was a part of me that thought I could make a little bit of amends. That, and I didn't want that money gettin' thrown out in the trash. I'd worked hard for it, and I thought Bonnie should have it.

"I went in the general store and glanced at the stack of

newspapers, prepared to bolt if I saw myself on the front page. I didn't see myself, so I grabbed a stack of moon pies and a five-cent postcard next to the register. I asked the clerk to add a postcard stamp to my order and asked if I could borrow the pencil by the register. I put Mike's address on the postcard and kept my note short and to the point.

"Please check the gray sock on the shelf in the garage. I'm so sorry.

"I set the pencil down, walked out of the store and dropped the postcard in the mailbox out front before finding a spot outside of town to eat my moon pies and get some rest. I like to tell myself that she used that money to buy a nice big headstone for Mike."

"Do you know why you couldn't bring yourself to go back and get the money Mr. Carr?"

"Yeah, I just told you why. I was a coward, and I didn't want to have to face his widow and sons."

"It's because you have a conscience. It's because deep down you are a good person, and you put Mike's family's needs before your own. That's what good people do."

"I don't know about all that, but if I had a conscience, it was a guilty one and I thought I could buy some peace of mind. If what I did was a good thing, as you say it was Padre, it was the last time in my life I had any good left in me."

XXVII

"I spent the next several months working my way east. At first, I would hide out during the day and travel at night. I honestly thought I was being pursued by the law. It wasn't much different than my journey south, from Iowa to Texas, except that this time I did my best not to interact with anyone and I didn't hop on any trains.

"I stole vegetables from gardens and used a few tricks that I'd learned while traveling previously. I'd check dumpsters behind cafes, restaurants and grocery stores. I could always find good food that had just been tossed out.

"I never strayed too far from the Gulf of Mexico. That's how I knew I was traveling east. The smell of damp, thick, sea air was always just over my right shoulder as I walked. I stayed a night or two in Lake Charles, LA and a few more nights in Lafayette. I continued east from there and did hitch a ride from a trucker who took me to New Orleans. That was quite a town, and I considered settling down for a while, but didn't think it was far enough from Galveston.

"I kept moving and started getting a little braver about hitching rides. It was early 1962 when a Texaco tanker driver dropped me off in Jacksonville, FL. This was as far east as I could go, and I decided maybe it was time to settle down in one spot for a while and see if I couldn't make a go at a normal life again.

"Jacksonville was a little different than Galveston. They had docks, but back then they weren't organized the same as Galveston. I tried getting a job, but didn't have any luck. I was able to get a few odd jobs here and there and check into a motel for a shower from time to time, but for the most part I was homeless, and I kept to myself.

"One old guy who owned a repair shop and gave me a little work here and there started asking me questions about who I was and where I was from. I still thought I was a wanted man, so I didn't tell him much. I guess he could tell that I was struggling and didn't want to talk, so he decided to tell me stories, with a little advice mixed in.

"He talked about all the different ways a young man could learn a skill that would earn him a living. I should have taken his advice and learned to be a mechanic or a welder, but I wasn't very excited about learning anything new right then, I just wanted a little security and to know that I wasn't wanted for Mike's murder.

"Mr. Ballenger realized pretty quick that I wasn't interested in educating myself and that the odd jobs he gave me weren't going to lead to any sort of long-term employment. He kept me around anyway and let me sleep on a cot in the back of the repair shop. I honestly don't remember how much he paid me, but I had a place to sleep, I could shower at the public beach shelters, and I could scavenge for food and buy a little whisky now and then. I really wasn't thinking about the future like I had been when I lived with Mike. I was just thinking about surviving through each week.

"Mr. Ballenger was in his late 60's at the time and his wife had already passed away and his kids were grown up and moved away. All he did at his repair shop was some oil changes, tire sales and minor repairs. He wasn't very busy and really didn't need my help with anything. I guess he kept me around for company more than anything else.

"One day he started talking about his service in World War I. He'd joined the Navy to avoid being drafted and his home base was here in Jacksonville. After the war he didn't reenlist and just decided to settle down and do the only thing he knew how to do. He had friends who had stayed in the Navy and progressed through the ranks.

"His repair shop became a rubber, oil and metal recycling shop during World War II, and he actually did quite well, but nowhere near as well as he'd have done if he would have made a career in the Navy. He sure as heck wouldn't still be coming to the shop every morning now if he had retired after 30 years in the US Military.

"So, I asked him,

"What would you be doing now Mr. Ballenger? If you had retired from the Navy?"

"Well, I'd do whatever the hell I wanted to do."

"It seems to me that you do whatever the hell you want to do now as it is."

"Listen Dan, you don't seem to understand what I'm telling you. You don't have any education that I'm aware of. You don't seem to have any desire to learn a skill or trade. You don't have any friends or family that you speak of. I really don't think you have any sort of plan for your life. It's really none of my business, but you know, the US isn't currently at war with anyone, and I think a career in the military would suit you well."

"So, over the next several months, Mr. Ballenger helped me get forms and documents I would need to prove that I was an actual person, and I joined the US Navy."

XXVIII

“Mr. Carr, it’s getting rather late in the afternoon. Do you need to take a rest? Would you like to nap for a bit?” Said Fr. Viloria.

“Padre, I’m almost afraid that if I sleep again, I might never wake up. And I really don’t care for the dreams I’ve been having when I do sleep. How ‘bout a little more water and I’ll keep talking until I doze off?” replied Dan.

“That will be fine. I imagine that you’re going to be getting to the part of your story where you will meet Malaya and find out she is pregnant soon and I want you to have the strength to tell me all about it.”

“You got that right Padre. It’s right around the corner. The last time in my life I was truly happy. And, just like every other time I was ever happy, it got ripped away from me.

“I hope you’re starting to understand why I’m such a miserable son-of-a-bitch. My entire life has been nothing but a waste of space and oxygen. I’ve honestly tried to do right from time to time, but I think I was just born cursed. Everything I’ve come in contact with has turned to shit.”

“Mr. Carr, I’ve been listening intently to you for two weeks now and I’m just not seeing the despair in your story. Hard times, tragedy, disappointment, unfortunate circumstances; yes, but really no more than the average person has endured over their lifetime. There has to be something I’m just not picking up on. I certainly don't want to minimize the sorrow and tough times you've had to endure, but I just don't see the utter hopelessness and misfortune in your life. You've been alive on this planet for 75 years. Every day that you wake up on the green side of the ground is a blessing. It's a day to celebrate. It's another chance to be a better man. Tomorrow can be that day for you, Mr. Carr. If you're still alive tomorrow morning, it's because God is giving you another chance. Your mission on earth is not yet complete."

"I'm not done with my story, Padre. Everything I've told you up until I joined the Navy could be chalked up to youthful indiscretions. As far as I could tell, I was just past my 16th birthday when Mr. Ballenger came up with the documents I needed to enlist.

"I think military life suited me, Padre. It gave me routine and stability. Three hots and a cot; as I said before. Back in those days there were a lot of us enlisted guys that had two options when it came to regular food and shelter; one was the military, and the other was prison. Some days there wasn't much difference between the two, but the military let me think I was a free man, making my own decisions, and they paid me regular money with no funny business.

"After basic and some specialized training, they even gave me a choice of which base I would be stationed at. I'd never been anywhere in my life outside of Iowa and wherever my legs could take me, so when I saw California on my list of choices, I knew that's where I was going.

"For four years I lived a pretty good life. I started to think that I found the place where I belonged. Us Navy guys kept hearing about the guys in the Army being sent to someplace called French Indochina, but as long as we could sandblast and paint ships in San Diego and head to the beach on the weekends, we really weren't too concerned about what was going on halfway around the world. Until it was our turn."

XXIX

"In summer of 1966 I had completed my four-year commitment, but it was the first time in my life that I felt like I belonged somewhere, so I re-enlisted for four more years. Hell, what 20-year-old kid wouldn't want the life I had? Do a little work during the day. Play cards and drink beer at night and go to the beach and hit on pretty girls and hook up all weekend. I honestly couldn't believe they paid me to do it. And they gave me food and housing on top of all that. I could have done that for the next hundred years.

"So, this went on for another year and I was one year into my second enlistment when they told my unit that we'd been reassigned, and we had a new mission. Our U.S. Seventh Fleet maintenance and repair unit was to report to an aircraft carrier that was headed to Asia. We ended up in some place called Sasebo, Japan at a US Navy base. We dropped off quite a few guys and picked up some others. My unit stayed on the carrier, and we headed south.

"Our carrier sat in the South China Sea for about 30 days at a time. The carrier would launch fighter jets to go bomb Vietnam and then we'd dock at the Subic Bay Naval Base in the Philippines to repair and replenish the ship and take a few days of R&R before heading back out."

"I am very familiar with Subic Bay Mr. Carr. I have never been there myself, but it is only about two hours from where I grew up in Manila. The U.S. Navy Base there is massive and provides many jobs to Filipinos."

"Yeah, well, I met one of those Filipinos who worked on the base. It was during our second port call. I'd seen her the first time working in the NEX at Subic, but didn't really give it much thought. I was interested in whiskey and sunshine on the beach. She was working the counter each day of our second port call as well and I managed to catch her eye and give her a wink and we traded smiles. The third time I decided that I'd chat her up a bit and see if it went anywhere.

"Malaya spoke much better English than I thought she would, and we chatted for about two minutes before her supervisor told me to get lost and quit bothering her while she was working. As me and my buddies headed out the door, no doubt to go drink rum on the beach, she held up four fingers. That was my cue to return at four when her shift ended.

"I stood outside the store and waited for her to come out. She came out and saw me, but didn't get too close. She was very shy and from a short distance away she gave me her address and said I would have to come to her home and speak to her father. I'd been drinking rum since noon and didn't think that speaking to her father right then would be a good idea, so I gave myself a few hours to get sober and then went to look her up."

"Oh yes, Mr. Carr. It seems your Malaya was a very traditional Filipino girl. Very shy and conservative. She would have still lived with her parents until she was married. And, you would have had to ask her father's permission just to speak with her, much less date her. Every young Filipino man has gone through this same exact exercise, and many American G.I.'s as well."

"Hang on now Padre. I sure as hell wasn't a grunt or a bullet sponge or a G.I. I may not have been much, but I was a Petty Officer Second Class making $278 a month after taxes. I was a hell of a catch, even if I was a drunk, uneducated redneck."

"I certainly didn't mean any disrespect Mr. Carr. Just pointing out the formal customs of dating in the Philippines."

"Yeah, well, it was certainly formal. I showed up at Malaya's parent's house and was not welcome. I stood on her front porch and talked to her father for at least 30 minutes, while she hid inside and peaked around the corner and smiled at me. If she hadn't done that, I probably would have just walked away. I caught on pretty quick that this whole thing was a game.

"I wanted to go out with her, and she wanted to go out with me and we were both plenty old enough to make our own decisions, but I had to play this shitty game with her father.

"So, I told her father all about growing up on a farm in Iowa. I sugar coated the shit out of my upbringing. I didn't tell him anything about my mom running away or my dad being a drunk and giving me and my brothers up or living in a barn. I made it sound like I was just a good, downhome, first-class American citizen. And I didn't tell him anything about the docks in Galveston.

"He asked me all about baseball and American muscle cars. Two things that I really didn't know crap about, but I knew enough to fake my way through his questions.

"On my third visit to her house, and after my third meeting with her father, she was allowed to come outside and sit on the porch with me while her father sat at the other end of the porch and pretended to read the newspaper.

"Padre, if I haven't already told you, Malaya was drop dead gorgeous. Way out of my league, but she seemed to like me, so I kept going back when we were in port. Occasionally her father would go in the house for a minute to get something and leave us alone on the porch. I was a horny 23-year-old and as soon as he went inside, I would try to hold her hand or kiss her on the cheek, but she wasn't having any of it.

"Finally, one day I stopped by to see her at work, and she said that her father gave her permission to go to the beach with me when she got off work at 4:00. He would give her until 6:00 and then come to pick her up. She brought a small basket of rolls and butter with her, and we sat on that beach and she fed me her homemade rolls until I was stuffed.

"My mind started thinking like it did back when I worked on the docks and lived in Mike's garage. I started thinking that maybe everything was going to be fine, and I could start planning for a future back home with Malaya. You know that little house with a little garage and pickup truck.

"We'd been seeing each other for about 6 months when my second enlistment ended. Malaya's father wasn't about to let me marry her and take her back to the US with me yet, so I had no choice but to reenlist, which I did, but for two years this time.

"I had two options, I could reenlist onboard the carrier that I worked on and continue 30+ days at sea and about 10 days in harbor, or I could ask for reassignment that would station me at the Subic Bay naval station permanently. It really wasn't even an option. The chance to see Malaya everyday was my choice.

However, for the reassignment reenlistment, I had to go to the Don Muang Royal Thai Air Force Base in Thailand to sign my reassignment papers.

I didn't want to leave. I wanted to sign my reenlistment and get on with my life with Malaya, but I also knew that my life with her was tied to my life in the US Navy and I had to do what they said. I had to go to Thailand and take some mandatory time off. Although I never saw battle, we were technically in a war and were required to leave the war zone every few years.

"Malaya and I had finally advanced beyond just looking at each other all googly-eyed and had done some pretty heavy petting and making out. I was afraid to try and go much further, thinking I might scare her away.

"During my final shore leave before my mandatory trip to Thailand, her father allowed us to spend an entire day together. It started out innocently enough; just our usual walks and talks and some holding hands and kissing. But, as the day wore on and it was getting closer to the time that I'd have to return to the base for my trip, we found ourselves on a little secluded area of the beach, just the two of us.

"Hunkered down amongst the rocks and tall grass and sand dunes we pressed our bodies close and the kissing and the petting got heavier and heavier until I thought I'd burst. That's when she said something I'll never forget.

"It wasn't particularly hot that day, but she had perspiration running down her neck and I was doing my best to keep up with kissing away the salty, steamy streaks. Her breathing was heavy, and she was grinding her pelvis against my thigh when she reached down and gently grabbed my crotch and, in my ear, she whispered,

"Please?!?"

"I wasn't sure I heard her correctly. I was caught a little off guard and backed away to look at her and register what she was saying. She pulled me back in, grabbed my crotch a little more firmly and whispered again with hot breath and a plea of desperation,

"Please Dan, please before you go!"

"I sure as hell wasn't going to make her ask a third time. I'd had my share of hookers and hookups in my life, but making love to Malaya on that beach back in the summer of 1969 was the first time in my life that I understood that this act was more than a biological function. It may not have lasted long, but it was the greatest three minutes of our young lives.

"We lay there in the sand, breathing heavy, dripping a little sweat and kissing each other lightly while the swelling in our groins went down and the blood returned to our brains. I promised her that I'd get to Thailand as quick as possible, sign my papers and do everything I could to return to her within a month.

"She had to be home before dark and I had to return to base, so I walked her home and gave her a quick peck on the cheek at the top of the porch stairs. Her father glared at me through the window, but the smile never left her face, and the glow never left her cheeks."

"That's quite a story Mr. Carr. And the way you tell it; maybe you should have been a writer or a storyteller."

"I should have been a lot of things Padre, but I wasted it all. I wasted my whole damn life feeling sorry for myself and feeling like I was the butt of some cruel joke. No matter what I did, it always turned out wrong and I finally got to the point that I quit trying. I got so fed up with life always kicking me and feeling like everyone else was getting some sort of deal that wasn't being offered to me. I got angry and bitter and decided to just 'fuck em all!'"

"Mr. Carr, something terrible must have happened from the time you and Malaya made love on the beach and the time she told you she was pregnant. It seems you were having a good life. You had stability, you had some money, you had a beautiful girlfriend who loved you. Please help me understand how that could be bad."

XXX

"I'm getting a little tired, but I'm afraid that if I go to sleep, I might never wake up."

"I understand your concern Mr. Carr. Your days here on earth are certainly few now. And your final days won't be spent telling stories. They'll be spent in a semi-conscious state of delirium. However, you do need to rest. Why don't you close your eyes? I promise I'll wake you in two hours."

"Pray hard for me Padre, just in case I don't wake up."

"Always Mr. Carr, always."

And Dan closed his eyes and immediately he dreamt.

He was back on the beach with Malaya, the love of his life. The two of them were watching the waves slowly roll in and crash against the sand. They sat on a blanket, with a picnic basket and an umbrella to block the intense rays of heat. Dan was happy to be back in the Philippines and spending time with Malaya. Two more years and certainly her father would allow Dan to marry her and take her back to the States.

Dan laid on the picnic blanket that day, more than 50 years ago, and pictured the small house he would buy. He pictured himself working on his truck in his small garage. He didn't know where they would live, and he really didn't care, just as long as the two of them were together.

Dan was deep in thought, becoming hypnotized by the sound of the waves, the puffs of clouds floating aimlessly above and thoughts of the future. He reached into the basket for another roll and Malaya leaned in close to him.

"Dan, my darling, I'm pregnant."

Dan turned and looked at her. He wasn't sure he heard her correctly. Malaya had a sweet, innocent smile on her face and she nodded her head.

"I'm not far along, but there's no doubt."

Dan smiled and sat up straight while turning to face Malaya.

"Are, are you sure? When did this happen? That day on the beach? Or, since I've been back? How far along are you?"

Malaya continued to nod and smile.

"So many questions Mr. Carr! Yes, I am sure. It most likely happened that day on the beach before you had to go to Thailand. You've only been back less than a month. I wouldn't know yet if it happened after your return."

"So, so you're about two months along?"

"Yes, most likely."

"Let's get married, Malaya. This baby is going to have a proper mother and father and I'm ready. I love you sweetheart."

"Not so fast Dan. My parents don't know, and my father isn't going to take this well. I'm fairly certain that he will have a bad reaction."

Mr. Carr? Mr. Carr? It has been two hours, Mr. Carr. Would you like to wake up and tell me more of your story?

Dan struggled to open his eyes. His mouth was dry and sticky, and his head was pounding. He tried to respond to Fr. Viloria, but all he could muster was a weak groan.

Fr. Viloria dabbed his lips with the wet sponge and Dan slowly licked the droplets. He coughed weakly and his chest rattled, and his throat grunted.

Dan knew that he had to finish the story. The next time he slept might be permanent.

XXXI

As had become the routine, Fr. Viloria swabbed some water on Dan's lips and tongue. Each time he woke it took a little longer for Dan to find his voice and begin to speak.

"Father, Dan creaked, "I'm quite certain that if you hadn't woke me, I would have continued that amazing dream until the Reaper decided to just shut my brain off.

"My dream picked up where my story left off earlier. I'd been back from Thailand for about a month and had my reassignment to Subic Bay naval station. I could see Malaya almost every day after work and always on the weekends.

"She invited me to her parent's house for Sunday dinner each week. Her father and I hadn't exactly become friends, but he didn't look like he wanted to rip out my heart and feed it to me anymore.

"Her mother was a sweetheart. She liked me. She always made sure I had a second helping of everything, and she served me dessert first. That pissed off Malaya's father and her mother knew it. My favorite dessert was something she called Turin. It looked like one of those deep-fried rollup things you get at the Chinese buffet that has vegetables in it, only these had bananas and brown sugar. Ohhh Lordy, I could eat a dozen of those."

"It's pronounced Turon Mr. Carr, said Fr. Viloria.

"Before I was adopted, I do remember a few things from the

orphanage. One of those being our Sunday evening meals when we would get dessert. Turon was always one of my favorites as well."

"Well things were going great. I had no doubt in my mind that Malaya wouldn't be coming home to America with me when my two years was up. Her mother liked me, her father didn't hate me and me and Malaya were madly in love with each other.

"I guess that's why it was such a kick in the gut the way things went down. I'm going to save the details of the day she told me she was pregnant for myself and my dreams, but I can tell you that I was happy as hell. I was ready to be a father, and I was ready to marry Malaya.

"I knew she loved me, and I knew she would have wanted to get married, but she was afraid of what her parents were going to say."

"So, what happened?" asked Fr. Viloria. If you both were so in love and having a baby together, why do you think things didn't work out?"

"It was her father. She wanted to tell her parents on her own and then would invite me over to dinner at the house to sit down with them and discuss our future plans.

"So that day on the beach, when she told me she was pregnant, she asked me to give her a few days to find the right time to tell them and then she would contact me.

"Four days later I couldn't stand it any longer. I went to her house and knocked on the door. Her father answered and just glared at me. I asked to talk to Malaya. He said she was gone. He said I shamed their family. He told me to leave and never come back.

"I tried to ask him where she was, and he slammed the door in my face. I knocked on the door. I looked in the window. I pounded on the door. I yelled into the house. I wanted to see Malaya and talk to her. I needed to know where she was.

"Her father called the police and had me removed from the front porch. I wasn't in any mood to be removed from the porch and ended up with a knot on my head and a night in jail.

"I had to be bailed out by my commanding officer, and he wasn't very happy about it. He took me back to base and told me I was confined there for 48 hours. I took that time to write a letter to Malaya.

"When my confinement ended, I went straight to her house. This time her father wouldn't even answer the door. I knew they were home, but they ignored me until I became too belligerent and then called the police again.

"I slipped the letter for Malaya through the mail slot in the front door and agreed to leave quietly. Not because I cared about jail or being confined to base, but mainly because I didn't want another knot, or worse, on my head from the police nightsticks.

"I went back to base and thought I'd work for a couple of days before I tried Malaya's house again. I knew if she was home, she would talk to me. I spent this time writing her more letters.

"I decided that Tuesday would be a good day to give her house another try. But on Monday I got papers delivered to me on base. Her father filed a restraining order against me, and I wasn't allowed within 100 feet of their house. My C.O. delivered it to me.

"He put two and two together that the knot on my head and night in jail must be related to the restraining order. He strongly suggested that it would be in my best interest, and the best interest of the US Navy, if I don't violate the order.

"I didn't know what to do. All I wanted to do was see Malaya and know that she was okay. I wanted to know that she was safe. She was having my baby, and I needed to know that she was okay."

Tears tried to well up in Dan Carr's eyes as he spoke. Due to his severe dehydration, very few tears formed, and his eyes just itched instead. Dan blinked repeatedly at the pain this caused and swallowed hard at the catch in his throat.

"I just wanted to see her again. I wanted to know she was okay. I wanted to know what happened to my child."

Fr. Viloria spoke, "Mr. Carr. The Philippines was and still is a predominantly Catholic country. Even today, but especially 50 years ago; an unmarried, pregnant woman would be considered a source of shame for a Filipino family.

"I can't speak to exactly what happened, but it's most likely that her father sent her away to a convent to have the baby. It would have been put up for adoption and your Malaya would have come home to her family and continued the path that her father had set out for her."

"Yeah, I'm pretty sure that's what happened. I kept writing letters and would walk by her house from time to time, hoping to see her there. I never did.

"I finished out my two-year enlistment and was done. In two years, she had never replied to a letter, and I had never caught a glimpse of her at the house. There was nothing left for me to do. I returned to the U.S. a broken man."

XXXII

Dan Carr was exhausted; mentally, emotionally and physically. He felt certain that he was ready to die.

"That's it Padre. That's the end of the story. I never heard from Malaya again. I returned to the US angry, bitter and uninterested in trying to be a good man.

"I spent my time working shitty jobs for shitty pay and blowing my paycheck at the bar, where I could always drag something home for a night or two.

"I tried marrying one or two of them, but I never gave it an honest effort. I knocked up a few more. I've never had much to do with any of my kids and they don't really want anything to do with me.

"I've pretty much fucked up the last 50 years of my life by not giving a shit about anything. You'd have to be one hell of a priest to get my worthless ass to heaven."

"Mr. Carr, I've told you that our God is a forgiving God. You only have to ask forgiveness for your sins to be granted access to heaven.

"You've told me your life story; and I understand that you're not satisfied with where you are today, but I don't think you're as bad of a man as you think. I'm sure you would choose to do some things differently if given the chance, but you're not the monster you make yourself out to be."

"Padre, there's a good chance that today, or tomorrow, or the next day will be our last conversation. I know my time is short and I'm ready for whatever comes next.

"I'll pray. I'll ask for forgiveness, and I know you'll do the same for me. But, if our God can grant miracles, I'd sure as hell like a do over.

"I'd like to take everything that I'm feeling right now and everything that I've learned during my life and be reborn," sniffed Dan Carr.

He was choking back tears and gasping for air in his weakened condition as he continued, "I know I could do better Padre. I know I could be a better man. It doesn't matter where I was born or how I was raised or how many bad things happened to me; I know that I could be a better man in this world and do good things.

"What do you think Padre? Can our God give me another chance?"

XXXIII

Fr. Viloria let Mr. Carr's hand down gently on the bed. Dan was asleep. Fr. Viloria knew that this may have been the last time they would talk.

Fr. Viloria climbed into his bed across the room but couldn't sleep. He hoped he would hear from his sister in the morning and then have just one more opportunity to talk with Mr. Carr.

XXXIV

It was still dark outside when Fr. Viloria climbed out of bed and looked at his roommate. Dan's chest was still rising and falling, although very slow and shallow.

Fr. Viloria showered in the tiny hospital room bathroom and prepared himself for the day. He made his way down the elevator to the hospital cafeteria and was getting a cup of coffee when his phone rang. It was his sister. Fr. Viloria set the half-filled cup of coffee on the counter and half-walked/half-ran out of the cafeteria while answering his phone.

"Yes. Yes, it's me. Hold on a second."

Fr. Viloria ran through the lobby and out the front doors. He stopped when he reached the edge of the parking lot and put his phone to his ear.

"Yes, please. What did you find out?"

Fr. Viloria listened intently. He nodded his head up and down and his eyes widened. A smile came across his face just before tears welled up in the corners of his eyes and rolled across his cheeks.

"Yes! Yes! Thank you so much! I love you and I'll see you soon!"

Fr. Viloria sprinted back toward the front door and across the lobby to the elevators.

XXXV

Fr. Viloria exited the elevator on the 5th floor and ran down the hallway toward room 514. He stopped at the nurse's desk and asked if Mr. Carr was awake yet. The nurse replied that the aide checked his vitals 20 minutes ago and he was still asleep.

Fr. Viloria continued down the hall and entered the room. Dan Carr looked so small and frail. He was certainly near death, but Fr. Viloria prayed that he had enough left in him for one more conversation.

Fr. Viloria approached the bed and put his hand on Dan Carr's arm.

"Mr. Carr? Mr. Carr? Can you wake up?"

Dan Carr groaned and grimaced. At least he wasn't dead.

"Mr. Carr? Please, I must speak with you. Can you hear me?"

Dan struggled to wake up. He blinked his eyes a few times and tried to lick his dry, chapped lips with his dry, sandpaper tongue.

"I'm here Padre. Just barely. I don't know if I'll be here tomorrow."

"Mr. Carr, said Fr. Viloria, fighting back sobs.

"I'm so glad that you are still alive. I have something very important to discuss with you. Can you open your eyes and let me know you're here with me?"

"I'm trying. I'm here and I'm trying to open my eyes. They don't want to cooperate."

"Take your time Mr. Carr. Take your time. I'm just so happy that you're still alive."

Fr. Viloria dabbed the sponge on Mr. Carr's lips and tongue. Dan licked his lips and cleared his dry, constricted throat. Fr. Viloria then went to the sink and turned on the hot water and began soaking a washcloth. He returned to the bed and washed Dan's face and eyes. He dabbed his lips once more with the sponge and Mr. Carr began to focus his eyes and clear his throat.

"Padre, I'm pretty sure that if you hadn't woke me up, I would have just drifted away into nothing. It's close now."

"I understand Mr. Carr and that's why I felt it was important to wake you. I have some news that I learned from my sister that you need to know while you still can."

"Okay? What's the news?"

"Do you remember two weeks ago when I went to see my sister and was gone for a few days?"

“Was that just two weeks ago? It seems like forever ago.”

“Yes, it was just two weeks ago. Not even two weeks actually. But there was a reason I went to see her. You started telling me your story and it made me wonder.”

“Wonder bout what?”

“Well, Mr. Carr, I grew up in an orphanage in the Philippines. My parents adopted me when I was an infant. I have always known that. They have always been honest with me that I was adopted. My sister, who is older than me, is the biological child of my parents, but she is my sister none the less.

“She moved to the US first and encouraged me to move here when I finished seminary. She is very special to me and we are very close.”

“Okay, said Mr. Carr.

“What are you getting at?”

“The Philippines makes it very difficult for orphans to ever figure out who their birth parents are. And honestly, I thought about it from time to time, but never pursued finding out. But then you started telling me your story. And I wondered. And I took one of your hairs and gave it to my sister. She works for a company that does DNA analysis.”

“Okay. I’m not sure what you’re getting at Padre.”

“Mr. Carr, the timeline adds up. Your Malaya told you she was pregnant in the summer of 1969. She would have had the baby in early 1970. She would have given the baby up for adoption.”

Fr. Viloria paused. Tears filled his eyes. He gripped Dan Carr's hand and took a deep breath.

"Mr. Carr, as I stand here today, I can't recall a happier moment in my life. I've been given the opportunity to hold the hand of my father as he leaves the physical world and enters the spiritual life for eternity."

"What in the heck are you talking about Padre? Whose father's hand are you holding?"

"Mr. Carr. Dan Carr. Father. Your Malaya is my mother. Your children are my siblings. You are my father. My sister's company does DNA analysis. I gave her one of your hairs and one of mine. Hair testing isn't the best method, but it's more than 80% accurate. How else could that be explained? I was born in the Philippines. You were born in Iowa.

"Mr. Carr, we can do a cheek swab if you need to be convinced 100%, but I don't need that. I know. You are my father and God made this happen. He put you in my life and me in yours. We didn't meet by accident. God put us both here, right now, at this moment."

Dan Carr was fighting back tears. He didn't need a cheek swab. He knew. He let the tears flow. He gripped Fr. Viloria's hand as tightly as he could. He knew.

XXXVI

Dan closed his eyes tightly. His weakened and dehydrated body had no more tears to shed. In the quiet hospital room, as the sun began to rise above the horizon, casting a warm glow across the room, Fr. Viloria spoke with a catch in his throat while tears rolled down his cheeks.

"Mr. Carr, father, dad. You've been through hell and back. I don't care what mistakes you might have made in your life…I'm proud of the man I get to call dad."

Dan's weary eyes met Fr. Viloria's glistening eyes.

"All I ever wanted in life was for someone to be proud of me", replied Dan.

And he closed his eyes and laid his head back.

For the next few hours, neither man said anything. Fr. Viloria wanted to ask Dan to live for him, so he could build a relationship with his father before natural causes finally took him. Dan didn't have the strength to speak much or even open his eyes. But he was aware of Fr. Viloria's presence and as his physical strength waned, his emotional strength soared.

XXXVII

The day wore into the afternoon and finally a quiet evening. As the stars adorned the night sky, Dan's weakened voice broke the silence.

"Padre. Son, I have to know, can I be forgiven?"

Fr. Viloria smiled gently, "Father, forgiveness is a gift we give ourselves. It's time to let go of the weight that shackles your soul. Embrace the possibility of redemption, and you will find peace."

With those words, a sense of serenity washed over Dan. For the first time since he had woken up in the hospital, Dan thought he might like to live a little longer.

"Son, can you do me a favor? Can you ask the doctor if I still have a chance to live?" choked Dan.

A large smile emerged on Fr. Viloria's face as he hugged and kissed on the cheek the frail body of his father.

"Yes, yes! he exclaimed as he gripped Dan's hand and tears dropped to the bed cover below.

"I will go inform the doctor right now! Healing begins now!" said Fr. Viloria as he ran from the room and down the hallway.

XXXVIII

Even with the feeding tube reinserted, Dan didn't expect to get better. But as days turned into weeks, which turned into months, something inside him refused to quit.

Slowly, Dan's physical condition improved. Within a few weeks, he was eating real food and feeding himself. Then he was using a wheelchair to take himself to physical therapy and soon enough, he was walking the hospital grounds with his son.

In the final moments of his hospital stay, Dan stood at the front door of the hospital, preparing himself to step back into the world he so desperately tried to leave. Fr. Viloria joined him at his side.

"Not long ago you asked me a question, father. You asked if our God could give you another chance.

"This is your chance. This is what I prayed for you."

The two men smiled and hugged.

"I'll go get the car," said Fr. Viloria.

Dan stepped onto the sidewalk and the glare of the sun made him shade his eyes with his hand. On the other side of the parking lot was a woman. Dan couldn't make out the details, but she was wearing a dress and what looked like an apron. She had long hair flowing down her back. She was walking toward the open green space on the other side of the parking lot.

Dan walked slowly down the sidewalk toward the parking lot, trying to get a better glimpse of the woman. As he neared the end of the sidewalk, she was nearly 100 feet away. The woman turned to him, held out her hand and in his mind, he heard her speak.

"Danny, it's me, your mother. Come with me?"

Fr. Viloria pulled up to the curb and Dan walked towards the passenger door. Just before opening the door and getting in the car, Dan smiled, softly and sadly.

"Not yet, Mama," he whispered to the woman across the parking lot.

"I have things to do."

www.ingramcontent.com/pod-product-compliance
Lightning Source LLC
LaVergne TN
LVHW011030110826
845149LV00015B/3359

* 9 7 9 8 9 9 0 2 6 7 3 2 9 *